ALSO BY ANDERSON FERRELL

Where She Was

HOME FOR THE DAY

HOME FOR THE DAY

A NOVEL BY

Anderson Ferrell

ALFRED A. KNOPF
NEW YORK
1994

This Is a Borzoi Book
Published by Alfred A. Knopf, Inc.

COPYRIGHT © 1994 BY ANDERSON FERRELL
ALL RIGHTS RESERVED UNDER INTERNATIONAL AND PAN-AMERICAN COPYRIGHT CONVENTIONS. PUBLISHED IN THE UNITED STATES BY ALFRED A. KNOPF, INC., NEW YORK, AND SIMULTANEOUSLY IN CANADA BY RANDOM HOUSE OF CANADA LIMITED, TORONTO. DISTRIBUTED BY RANDOM HOUSE, INC., NEW YORK.

A PORTION OF THIS WORK ORIGINALLY APPEARED IN *The Quarterly*.

GRATEFUL ACKNOWLEDGMENT IS MADE TO THE FOLLOWING FOR PERMISSION TO REPRINT PREVIOUSLY PUBLISHED MATERIAL:
NEW DIRECTIONS PUBLISHING CORP.: EXCERPT FROM "ASPIRATION" FROM OCTAVIO PAZ, *COLLECTED POEMS 1957–1987*, TRANSLATED BY ELIOT WEINBERGER, COPYRIGHT © 1988 BY OCTAVIO PAZ AND ELIOT WEINBERGER. REPRINTED BY PERMISSION OF NEW DIRECTIONS PUBLISHING CORP.
SONY MUSIC PUBLISHING: EXCERPT FROM "I FALL TO PIECES" BY HARLAN HOWARD AND HANK COCHRAN, COPYRIGHT © 1960 (RENEWED) BY TREE PUBLISHING CO., INC. ALL RIGHTS ADMINISTERED BY SONY MUSIC PUBLISHING, 8 MUSIC SQUARE WEST, NASHVILLE, TN 37203. ALL RIGHTS RESERVED. USED BY PERMISSION OF THE PUBLISHER.

LIBRARY OF CONGRESS CATALOGING-IN-PUBLICATION DATA

FERRELL, ANDERSON.
　HOME FOR THE DAY: A NOVEL/BY ANDERSON FERRELL.—1ST ED.
　　P.　CM.
　ISBN 0-394-58094-X
　　1. FATHERS AND SONS—SOUTHERN STATES—FICTION.　2. GAY MEN—SOUTHERN STATES—FICTION.　3. DEATH—FICTION.　I. TITLE.
PS3556.E7257H66　1994
813'.54—DC20　　　　　　　　　　　　　　　　93-45301
　　　　　　　　　　　　　　　　　　　　　　CIP

MANUFACTURED IN THE UNITED STATES OF AMERICA
FIRST EDITION

FOR DIRK LUMBARD

Strike your flint, burn, memory,
Against the hour and its undertow.
—OCTAVIO PAZ

For their guidance and generosity, I thank these people—my editor, the brilliant and thorough Gordon Lish, Kenneth and Anne Collins Barnes, Liz Darhansoff, Agnes de Mille, Jonathan Sheffer, and Bruce Sussman.

I am grateful to The National Endowment for the Arts for its support of this book.

HOME FOR THE DAY

If MY DADDY wants to shoot me he'll have to come here. He wouldn't let me come into his house, not even to shoot me. So, if he means to do it, it will have to be right here, in this graveyard.

It's been a year, and a spring and a summer after that since I did what made him want to kill me today. Over two years since I found the place again and got everybody interested in helping me to clean it off.

It's the only place I wanted to come to after what happened.

The local law states that I can be here until sundown. I could probably stay until after dark. I doubt that the local law would come out this far, and this is a family cemetery, private, so the local law may not apply.

But I won't stay until after dark. I'll leave in time to catch the plane back to New York City. Between now and then there is enough time to figure out if I want to make my daddy see that he wouldn't have tried to shoot me if he didn't love me.

What I don't know is whether or not my daddy really

wanted to shoot me. I was in the clear there in his front yard. He could have fired from inside the house—gotten me before I knew what had hit me. Right away he could have shot me clean and cold. I wouldn't have seen him do it, wouldn't have seen how it was going to be. There would have been no time to try to save myself, to try to talk him out of it. It could have been quick and clear for me. It would have been over by now. I wouldn't be sitting here trying to think what I am trying to think.

But he didn't do it the clean way. He stepped out onto his front stoop where I could see him, cocked his shotgun, the one his daddy had given him, and aimed at me. I am trying to think that the reason my daddy fired over my head instead of into it is that he loves me so much.

Not that I wish he had shot me dead. I am still glad he didn't. What I wish is that it hadn't happened the way it did. What I wish is that I knew what I'm supposed to take it as— that shot over my head. What I wish is that he hadn't come out of the house with his daddy's gun.

But it is my daddy himself who has always said that I want things the way I want them. It is my daddy who used to tell me to want in one hand and spit in the other one and see which hand gets full first. It was also my daddy who said that I usually get things just the way I want them.

When he stepped out of the house onto his front stoop and raised his daddy's gun and cocked it and aimed at me, I forgot what it was that I had done. I asked him.

"You think about that," he said. Then Daddy fired. The blast surrounded me, then in the air behind me I heard a tight pop. When I turned to run I saw the power line quivering across the steet. I saw that there was nowhere to go.

Nowhere to hide, just the empty street and an open field in front of the house. Sky above. "How come you thought I wouldn't know?" Daddy shouted.

I turned back around ready to be filled.

But Daddy was gone.

I'LL THINK about it here. If that is what my daddy wants, that's what I'll do. Here in this quiet, still place I'll get it straight.

First there is a grave I want to see. The grave I want to see is in the corner farthest from the gate. It is right up against the back fence, and is unmarked. The weeds are high and a maze of tombstones stands between me and that grave. I cannot see it from where I am, but I know it is there.

It is a hard walk over to that far corner of the graveyard. They cleaned the place off again a little over a year ago, but I was not here. That cleaning seems to have made the soil less weary, for the weeds grow thicker and healthier than how I remember them from before. By the time I reach the grave my trouser legs are stiff with beggar's-lice and sheep burs.

Though the grave is a year old nothing has grown on it. The dirt is a sunny-colored mix of clay and sand, and the grave itself is smaller than the others, looks more as though a little dog or a baby is buried there, but it is not mounded, which makes it look as old as the oldest graves here. On the day I dug it, and put Pete's ashes in it, I was careful to smooth it over and make it look, if not undetectable, as if it belonged. After a year of rain and wind the marks I raked are still there, duller than that day a year ago. But they are there. When I get down and touch the grave I feel the dirt has formed a thin shell, but I break it with my fingers and find the soil beneath the crust is as soft as talcum powder. I lean over and put both palms flat onto the grave and just feel it. I am alone. I don't cry. I don't want to, unless it would either kill me or bring him back. And I know now, after a year, that it will do neither. So, I will stay here until sundown and think about what I have done. I'll go back over everything up to this point, and if there is a difference between how I see it and how I want it to be seen, I will tell it.

I AM THE FOOL who got everybody interested in this place again. Until twenty years ago it had been the burying place of my family, then it filled up, and we started putting our people in the town cemetery, where somebody else would tend the graves for us. I was sixteen when that happened, and I did not see the place again until a day in early spring two years ago when I was home for a visit and thought up the graveyard as a way of getting out of the house for a while.

To find out how to get here that day I had to go ask my grandmother.

"It's way out close to the county line," she said. She is my mother's mother and lives across the town in a better house than my daddy's. None of her blood kin is buried here, but it is in her nature to keep up with anything that she thinks might get forgotten, and she likes when, after a time, people do the right thing. She likes to see right prevail, but she enjoys as well her great pleasure, which is pointing out how long it takes. When I asked her the way to the graveyard, she raised her hands and looked up as though heaven were right where it should be—above her kitchen ceiling—and she said she was glad somebody was finally taking an interest in the place again.

Her directions were not easy to follow. The turns she had marked in her mind by old home places of people she had known when she was young. The roads I would need to take she had named herself according to what churches were on them or what creeks their bridges crossed. But the start was simple and clear. I understood it.

"Take the road to Macala, and when you get to the first right, turn right right there," she said.

I DROVE UP the path as far as I could, then I had to stop the car and walk the rest of the way.

The graveyard then was overgrown, as it is now—a tangle of blackberry brambles and knee-high in broomstraw. The rusted iron gate, having been left open a long time ago, could not be closed. A pine tree had grown up by the gate, and the post and hinges had become embedded in the tree trunk. There were thorny, dried vines hanging in the trees and twisting like barbed wire along the fence.

I had not remembered so many graves, and, there being no new graves, it looked as though my family had stopped dying. The place was so grown-over that it made me think perhaps they had discovered the secret of everlasting life, and that had allowed them to banish from their minds all thoughts of death and remembrance and obligations to graves. Or really that we had all died off long ago. It was quiet and so peaceful.

I came in, and picked my way around the briers and sweet

gum saplings. I read every stone that had anything on it to read. I started in the center with the oldest graves, which are marked by nothing but plain granite stobs put there at a time when people built a box, dug a grave and buried their dead with their own hands in ground which they alone tended. I found no names and dates on these stones. The mourners and rememberers of the long dead could not read or write, I reasoned. But from other stones I scraped dead moss and pulled dry vines to find that weather over time had worn away the inscriptions until only faint indentations remained—unreadable, as though carved in melting ice. And the people buried there? Unremembered, alone, unnamed.

Then I moved out from the center toward the more recent tombstones and memorials, properly carved with dates and names and sweet epitaphs. Then farther out, where lay the ones who had recorded the first dates, composed the first epitaphs, until I was at the place where pressed up against the rusty iron fence that holds in the dead, holds in the vines, holds in the trees planned and random, are the most recent graves. Scattered sprays of narcissus bloomed then up against some of the gravestones and in between the palings of the fence. Tufts of new grass and wild onion grew in between the wickets.

Now, the field surrounding the graveyard is knobby with plowed-under corn stubble, but that day it was harrowed smooth in preparation for planting, making the graveyard look like a place that, having been forgotten by those who should have cared for it, simply suited itself.

I sat down on the stone bench by the graves of Polly Ann and Benjamin Nathan Watson, beloved of each other, it says on their separate stones. The bench has an inscription stating it was placed there by Polly Ann herself only three months before the date of her death.

A breeze marbled the leftover winter cold with new warm air. Then the breeze stopped, and the sun felt good on the side of my face. There was a clear sky that day, as there is today. But then the air was light with the scent of tender green and wormy earth. So quiet. Not a ripple in sight. I lay down on the bench and fell asleep, and I did not dream.

A DOOR SLAMMED and woke me up. On the front porch of the house across the path, there was a woman. She waved, and I waved back to her. Then, she came off her porch and started toward me, quickstepping her way as though she were going to chase off a stray dog. When she got to the fence she stopped. I stood up, for I always behave in a fine way around people who I don't think would know fine ways, and it is a flaw in me that I decide too quickly about women like this one. I don't behave in this fine way for the right reasons, and it is no less a flaw just because I know it.

She acted as though I had not done anything too fine.

"Hey," she said.

"Good morning," I said.

"Hey," she said again. She looked to be in her fifties. Her hair was short and black and had been recently fixed in an outdated style—curled, ratted a bit, then smoothed out and sprayed with lacquer. She wore glasses with silver rims around the bottoms of the lenses and two slashes of black plastic above that looked like over-made-up eyebrows. It was what Grandmother would call a Baptist face, a Primitive Baptist face—hard and holy. She was wearing a pant suit in a blue color like no blue she could ever have come across in natural things, and a white blouse that buttoned up the front and was printed with mailboxes on posts. A few sprigs of grass sprouted around the posts, and a bluebird was perched on each mailbox. Two little musical notes were balanced on the end of each bluebird's beak.

"You going to clean that place off?" she asked.

"I beg your pardon?" I asked.

She folded her arms and nodded toward the graveyard. "You going to clean that place off?" she asked again. "I love to see people look after dead folkses' graves."

I told her I was just here for a visit. "I don't live here," I said.

She walked over to a clump of narcissus that was growing by the gate, leaned forward, and lifted her head so as to examine the flowers through the strong part of her glasses. "Somebody ought to clean this place off," she said. She bent over from her waist and started pulling weeds from around the narcissus. I watched her hands dance in the dirt.

"Well, I would clean it off, but I don't live here. And I think the place has a kind of charm, actually," I said.

"Not to me," she said. "I don't see nothing charming about a graveyard, especially one as growed-over as this one. I guarantee you the charm would slip for you too if you had to live across from it." She straightened up, holding a handful of weeds she had pulled. Then she knocked the roots against the fence to clean off the soil and threw the weeds onto the hard-packed dirt of the path, where they could not take root. "It wouldn't be so bad if somebody got right on it before spring comes for sure and it grows up good-fashioned."

I said nothing, but sat back down on the bench. She stood by the gate and looked out across the empty field.

"I love to see people look after dead folkses' graves," she said.

"You'd have to talk to my daddy," I said.

"You're here, he ain't," she said, then she pushed against the gate but it would not close, and one of the iron palings came off in her hand. She shook her head slowly and said, "Lord 'a mercy," as though really to say what a sorry mess, nothing worse. We looked at each other for a moment, she with the iron rod in her hand as proof of everything she had said. I expected an apology, but she made none. Then, from the house someone hollered, "Estelle!"

I looked and saw a man standing in the doorway holding open the screen door.

"Your cabbages is boiling over," the man yelled.

"Well, turn down the heat!" she shouted to him. She leaned the paling against the gate and started back toward her house, then as though she had forgotten something, she turned around. For a moment she studied the piece of fence. Then she came back to the gate.

"Can I have that?" she asked.

I knew what she wanted. A woman like her can always use a piece of iron for something. "Yes, take it," I said.

She took the paling and went off toward her house. I watched her go back up the path, cross the yard, jump the ditch and land in her yard. She stopped by a stick of something she was trying to make grow, pushed the iron paling into the ground beside it and tied the rod to the branchless, leafless plant with some string which she had taken from her pocket.

The man had been holding open the screen door ever since he had called her, and he held it still while she climbed the porch steps and walked past him into the house. I saw the door swing shut behind her, and heard it slap to. I sat for a little while longer on the bench, then I got up, walked down the path to where I had left the car and drove, not home, but to my grandmother's house.

"I TOLD THEM ALL, every last one of them, that it had to be done," Grandmother said, taking from the oven a plate of food that she had put aside for me. "Told them it just couldn't wait. Now is the time, I said, before everything buds up and starts to sprout and it gets snaky down there." She put the food on the table in front of me—two fried chicken legs, shriveled like water-soaked fingers, some boiled string beans and a mound of mashed potatoes, crusted over like old snow. She poured a glass of iced tea and set it by my plate. Then she went to the other end of the table where she had a towel laid out and the iron plugged into the light cord that dangled from the ceiling. She has ironed in this way as long as I can remember, preferring it to dragging down the ironing board, as she says. From a brown paper bag, wrinkled and fuzzy with use, filled with a tangle of colors, she pulled, hand over hand like the magician's trick with the endless scarf, a ribbon of organdy cloth. It was as knotted and wrinkled as crepe paper.

"We could burn that graveyard off, see," she said, picking the knots loose. "All the dead grass and briers and broomstraw. On a Saturday. Make a party of it." She finished untangling the ribbon, hung it around her neck and went to the sink. She got the spray starch from the cabinet under the sink, then she came back to the table and with her free hand turned the iron up. The light dimmed and three seconds were ticked off somewhere inside the iron. She put one end of the ribbon onto the towel, and separating the wrinkles with her fingers, sprayed the ribbon with the starch. She pressed the iron down on the material. The hot metal on the wet organdy made a sound like a cat sneezing. When she lifted the iron again the end of the ribbon was splayed out flat against the towel, showing its colors and design—a crisp stripe of each kind in a rainbow. She peeled away the part she had done and moved another length as long as the iron was wide. When she had finished ironing it, she rolled up the organdy ribbon, put a rubber band around it and placed it in a fresh paper bag taken from the supply of fresh paper bags she kept in the kitchen safe. It was something I had seen her do before. I knew this bag of ribbons, each and every one. It is her habit, formed when I was a child, to keep them starched and ironed, for when I was a small boy they were one of my favorite toys. I made maypoles with them, wore them, ran with them, nearly ruined them. When I would finish playing with them, I'd gather them up by the handful and cram them back into the bag. She never scolded me, but would patiently take the bag down and press the ribbons out, roll them up and put them away where they would remain until I dragged them out again on some rainy, boring day. From me she got the belief that children like to play with them. She shows the bag and its colorful contents to all the children who visit her, and if they wish to she lets them play with the ribbons as I did.

"And what else I said was that it was a disgrace the way it is right now," she said. "What did they think the other people think? The ones that live across from it, I asked them. Their yard and fields looking like just the right way a yard and fields ought to look. And *that* flopped down in the middle of it." She pushed her glasses up from the end of her nose with the back of her wrist. "It reflects," she said. "Don't think it don't."

Such a thing so small as pushing up her glasses changed her face, and though not made to look younger, her face was lifted, surer, sure, as sure as starch, ironed.

I drank down what was left of my tea, then took the glass and plate and silverware to the sink. I started to leave the kitchen and go out to the porch to sit and swing and wait to see how long it could be that nothing would happen. But before I went, I kissed my grandmother on the cheek and smelled powder and menthol and let the smell and the face hold me there in the kitchen. I had gotten as far as the door though, before I let myself stay. Then I turned around and leaned on the door jamb and thought, let's do it, let's see who knows what.

"Why does it reflect, if it does?" I asked her. "Why does it?"

From the old bag she took another ribbon, purple moiré. "That is not any kind of a question at all. 'Why does it reflect?' " she said, turning the iron down to a cooler setting for the moiré. "No doubting about that it reflects, and why it reflects is not what you want to know. If you have a question it is this. Do you care that it reflects?"

"I would if I thought it did," I said.

She put one end of the purple ribbon onto the towel and pressed the iron down on it. Then she pulled the remaining length of ribbon under the iron with a graceful flourish, drawing her arm back and out as though raising it to strike. The ribbon, creased and wrung, slithered from one side of the table, under the iron, then raced out from under the other side, shiny and flat, until the whole length of it flipped into the air over her head then floated back to the table like a trail of descending purple smoke.

"What you think won't change what I know," she said. "And besides, you've got it wrong and backwards. You've got to care first." She put the purple ribbon away and reached deep into the old bag, up to her elbow without looking. She brought out a red ribbon of real satin. "Isn't this pretty?" she asked. "It's from a time before they started making them from acetate. And such a pretty color. The florists call it 'Better Times.'" She started working on the red ribbon, doling it out onto the towel, straightening and pressing, the iron releasing a steamy, starchy smell, and the smoothed ribbon inching its way across the table toward me. Then, when she had ironed about two feet of ribbon, a glue stain in the shape of a curly-handled *H* appeared. The light from the bare bulb above caught in some specks of silver glitter which were caught in the weave of stained satin where the glue had been, and as she ironed, more faint, light-dusted letters came out. *U*, then *S*, on and on until a whole word lay on the table between us, and the word was *HUSBAND*. When she had finished she took the ribbon up, holding it out in front of her, letting lengths of it fall over the backs of each hand like a priest holding the stole out before he ties together the hands of the bride and groom.

I CALL IT a straight house, the brick veneer, ranch-style with a carport, where my daddy and mother live. The straight house sits among others like it on the outskirts of town on land that used to do better with corn, cotton, tobacco. The streets in this part of town are new and unpaved.

HOME FOR THE DAY

The houses become coated inside and out with fine dust if crankcase oil is not sprinkled on the streets now and then. There are no trees higher than any of the houses even though everybody has planted the fast-growing kind: silver maple, mimosa, pine. Unless good dirt is hauled onto a lot, nothing nice will grow—not ivy nor azaleas nor boxwood nor oak. Drainage is a problem. The ground is mushy and stinking over septic tanks. In hot weather, walking barefoot across the backyards is unhealthy. There are no garages and not enough storage space in the houses, so the carports serve as attics and pantries. It is a general thing to see a rust-dappled deep freezer under many of the carports. Yards are strewn with miniature tractors and toy cars made of once brightly colored plastic now faded from being left outside in the weather.

The dirt street stops at my daddy's house and beyond that is a field, still cultivated, in the middle of which is an old tenant dwelling, where in summer migrant workers are housed. Then, finally, edging the field are some nice woods.

The straight house has next to nothing of what I like in a house. There is no parlor or dining room, but instead a room where you do everything but cook and sleep—a room which the people who build straight houses call a great room. What I like in a house are halls and rooms, a place for eating that is separate from the kitchen, a proper dining room. And I like a place just for sitting and talking which is full of nice things. I like a room in which to hide the television set. Porches are almost elegant, I think. The straight house has just the stoop from where my daddy shot at me.

When my daddy and mother first moved into the straight house I tried to get them to turn the carport into a den with a fireplace and bookshelves. I told them they should divide up the kitchen and make a proper dining room.

"I don't want nothing to do with a filthy fireplace," Daddy said, when I suggested my ideas for improving the place. "This house is exactly what I want. Easy to keep warm, and it don't ramble."

I shouldn't have cared about this straight house. It was never what I thought of when I thought of home. I took my meals there and came and went, but I only occasionally slept under my daddy's roof. Where I slept most often was across town with my grandmother, who paid me two dollars a week to be there in case she fell or got sick in the night. It is from her that I picked up the term straight house. That is what she calls all houses like my daddy's, and she looks down on the people who build them only a little less than she looks down on the people who live in them. She lives in what, with pride, she calls a big, old, rambling, hard-to-heat place. But I did care about my daddy's house. I did want to make it ramble a little. I wanted it to look like a place where I might live, and as I had plans for leaving the town as soon as possible, I wanted a place to come back to that looked like a place I had come from.

There is a place that looks as if I came from it. It is the big, rambling house owned by my grandmother. It is her house on a street planted long ago with oak trees in the old part of town that is my notion of a place suitable to be the place from where I came. In the yards of the houses that line the street flourishes everything that will not grow around straight houses. Azaleas have to be trimmed yearly, and the cuttings are given to friends. From boxwood she has grown, my grandmother has a wreath made for every door and window of her house each Christmas. Every house on the street has an old stable behind it that is used now as a garage, and many of the houses have other outbuildings, old washhouses converted to guest quarters or offices, acetylene light plants, smokehouses and potting sheds.

Grandmother's house sits on land higher than the street. There are cement steps up to the front yard and a paved walkway to her porch. The porch runs across the front and one side of the house with a gazebo built in at the corner. Her porch she calls the "pie-azza."

Inside the house there are two parlors on either side of a wide hall that runs the length of the house. The hall is paneled in oak, dark with polish, and the floors are oak as well. Above the paneling on white plaster walls are old photographs of relatives: great-grandfathers, my grandfather as a young man, widowed great-aunts up to their chins in black taffeta, huge mourning brooches swelling at their throats like goiter. The poses in the photographs are formal, and the photographs themselves are framed in heavy, ornately carved and gilded wood as though they were fine oil portraits. At the far end and to one side of the hall is a staircase with maroon carpet held in place on each step by a shiny brass rod. Halfway up to the second floor is a landing where on the wall is a print of a painting by Rosa Bonheur called *The Horse Fair*. I did not know while I lived there that the painting was a famous one or that it existed in any form other than that which it took at my grandmother's stair landing. And later, after I had left home and was living in New York City, I felt mildly outraged then somewhat prideful when I turned a corner and discovered the original hanging in the Metropolitan Museum of Art. Grandmother's print is half the size of the real thing, and it is, I guess, a sign of something not quite fine in me that the actual painting, hanging as it does, huge, colored and in proper light, had not the same power for me as the print in black and white on my grandmother's dark landing. There in her overly formal and somewhat funereal house with its polished oak drinking up what little light there is as though it were lemon oil, the print, with its turmoil of strong-armed farmers and wild-eyed, bridling draft horses, gives a sort of whore-in-church quality to the house—a reminder that passions checked need not lose their ginger. As I looked at it that day in the museum, I could not see in the real thing what my grandmother saw in her copy that made her have the print taken down and put away whenever the preacher came to supper.

The house itself was built around 1900 not by my grandparents, who in those days would not have had the money or the taste for such a house, but by the president of the Branch Creek Bank and Trust. When the bank failed during the Great Depression, my grandfather bought the house for a small amount of hard cash which he had kept for the times my grandmother said he'd seen coming. She told me how he had gotten the house and all the furniture for about half of what one year's tobacco crop had brought him. They quit farming, leased out their land and farmhouse to some white trash and moved into town. Grandfather bought a second-hand Packard and a dry-goods store and became, in my grandmother's words, "somebody who everybody had to deal with." They dealt, and, also according to my grandmother, they didn't like it. Grandfather's prices were fair but set in stone, and he gave credit to Negroes only, believing that white people had no excuse to ask for it. This policy did not go over well with white people, especially trash, and I'm told that this fact did not cause him a moment of concern. It is, I believe, the basis for my shameful disdain for people like that woman at the graveyard.

It was in this house and to these circumstances that my

mother was born, and it was back to the house that, after she married him, she brought my daddy and when I was born, me. Why she did it is in the story of it. It is a story I have heard her tell and that she has told me often, the point of which is my importance. So I took it, and so Mother meant it to be. She told me how before I was born, she and Daddy lived in an apartment over the funeral home where Daddy worked. He started out as a hearse driver just after they were married, Mother said. But he watched and helped and learned to embalm. The man who owned the funeral home liked my daddy so much and hated his own son so much that he was going to make Daddy his partner and, Mother thought, would have probably left Daddy the business eventually. All Daddy had to do was get certified. It was a good business, Mother said. And I know the man who runs it now is rich. Mother said Daddy would have gotten rich too, but when she found out I was coming she made Daddy quit the job because she didn't want me growing up over a funeral home. The man said the deal was off if Daddy couldn't live in the apartment so somebody would be there at night.

I wouldn't have minded if we had stayed.

We moved into the fine old place with my grandparents. We lived with them and their silver and china. Their furniture was good—old and expensive. We lived with fine things, and after some time, only those families in Branch Creek who had their own fine things knew that these were not my daddy's. But when the occasion called for it, when the remark was apt, my grandmother would say to Daddy and me, "This house has improved you some, but not enough," and the people from the families with their own fine things, I imagined, gave approving nods.

But to people who think a situation is what it looks like, ours certainly looked like what it was not.

IT HAS ALWAYS BEEN in my nature to cause small troubles in small ways, but it wasn't to make anybody feel obligated to care for the place that at one time I wanted to be buried here. Nor was it to set myself apart from those members of my family who would not be buried here. What it was, the reason, was that it seemed like a thing I would do, be buried in a place where there was room left for just one. It was an elegantly simple gesture, I thought, that was as telling as a grand one.

The reasons I liked it here then are the reasons why I like it still. Because it is old and because the fence is rusty but hasn't completely fallen. Under the cedar trees weeds don't grow and the graves there stay tidy and fragrant and even on a winter's day you can have a memory of summer in the shade of those evergreen branches. Those are the things which drew me here and the things which draw me still. It is pleasant here.

Only now I don't care whether I am buried or not. Still, the cedar trees are beautiful, shedding strips of silvery bark.

When we gathered to clean the graveyard off that time two years ago, there was talk of cutting down the cedars. They interfere with the fence, and it was thought by some that the fence would last longer if the trees were removed. One plan was to cut down all the trees, level off the ground, spray something that makes the soil completely barren and spread crushed white rocks over the whole place. Some wanted to leave the trees, do away with the fence and put up a low brick wall. Ambitious plans for new granite tombstones were made. The women leaned on their rakes and pointed out places for ornamental shrubs, and talked and gestured flower beds into existence in our minds. But soon the expense of such undertakings was considered by the few realists in the family, so in the end we just took out all the weeds, pruned the cedars a bit, repaired the fence where we could and left that which had over the years been done for us by time and the elements do for us still. This erosion of our resolve came about as a result of forgetfulness and distraction, but on that day when we first gathered to clean the place, and Uncle Fate, who once belonged to the Klan and knew how to control fire, sloshed gasoline over all the dried vines and young saplings, on the dead weeds at the base of the tombstones and along the fence, we were of a mind not just to clean and preserve the graveyard but to renovate it.

Uncle Fate threw a match into the weeds just by the gate and conjured a column of fire before our eyes that sprang up making the same sound as the cloth his wife was shaking out to spread on the tailgate of his pickup truck. He stuck his hoe into the blaze and drew a line of fire around the whole graveyard, and we all stood and watched as the line of fire became four red walls drawing in on themselves toward the center of the graveyard, burning everything that was not stone or iron or earth. And as the wall of fire receded, row after row of smoking tombstones appeared before it, as though they were marching out of the fire. Dead moss and lichen on the stones glowed red and then burned to ash and were blown away by the fire wind, revealing inscriptions in the stones, as though they had been written in magic ink. And the fire burned furiously in on itself and roared, and the vines and weeds popped and crackled and we all stopped whatever we were doing and watched and listened to the fire. It sounded like cattle stampeding through broken glass. It burned seemingly uncontrolled for a time, and it looked as though God's judgment was being handed out, years late perhaps, but hellishly, finally and on the spot. Then the four sides of the fire reached the center of the graveyard and swirled into a funnel higher than our heads before it went out as quickly as it had started.

I did very little of the work that day, not being handy with rake or hoe or bush ax. In truth, there was less work than I had expected, the fire being the most useful tool and very saving of labor.

The fire made us hungry, and we had to wait for it to stop smoldering anyway before we could do more work. The women finished laying out the picnic on the tailgate of Uncle Fate's pickup truck, and we all washed our hands in water he had brought in a ten-gallon drum which even had a built-in spigot. Several people remarked how it was just the very thing needed for such occasions as this, and Uncle Fate told how he had made it himself—cut a hole in the drum with his acetylene torch and welded the spigot in place. He had even thought to throw a few folding patio chairs into his truck for any of the women who didn't want to sit on the ground.

All the women had brought a little of the same things, so there was plenty to eat—fried chicken, ham biscuits, deviled eggs, sweet pickle relish—but the tastes were various as each woman had her own particular way of preparing the same dish.

It was a pretty sight, the picnic laid out on the tailgate, the pastel-colored plastic containers on the white cotton tablecloth. Aunt Fan, who likes to make centerpieces out of just about anything, cartwheels and hubcaps, cottonballs and tissues, had gone off to the ditch bank and found violets and vetch and wild daffodils and a pint whiskey bottle and made a bouquet for the tailgate.

"No reason it shouldn't be nice," she said, placing her handiwork on the cloth.

Then just when the picnic was laid and ready, Uncle Fate went into the cab of his truck and pulled out three grease-stained white paper sacks which we all recognized as being from the best barbecue place in the county. He took out four quart-sized cardboard containers from the bags and placed them among the homemade things. And several people let him know how they appreciated what he had done.

"I declare, Fate."

"You ought not to have done that."

"I'm sure glad he did."

Uncle Fate stood back smiling, and he waited until everybody had gotten some food before he went to the back of the truck to make himself a plate.

The graveyard was black and smoky, and we gathered by it for our picnic as though by a misty pond, some sitting on the new grass outside the fence, some standing, others sitting on the folding chairs.

In all, I counted twenty-five there that day. All of Daddy's brothers and sisters and their wives and husbands showed up. Before the day was out, every one of them but Uncle Fate had made a point of talking to me. How was New York, some asked, and wondered out loud how I could stand it, though the only one who had ever been was Uncle Thaddy, who had stopped there briefly on his way back from World War II. He didn't know how I could stand it either, but admitted that he would like to go back there for a longer visit sometime. And they told me of their children, my cousins, most of whom had married and were having children themselves; doing well, was what I was meant to think. Aunt Cathleen, short of breath with relief, told me that even my cousin Jack was married, and I could not help myself from laughing in her face, which she took for congratulations. I was remembering how he and I used to stage wedding processions up to the point where the groom entered, and how we argued over whose turn it was to wear the cheesecloth veil on his head. I remembered as well how, even as teenagers, we were still playing a game we called romantic fever whenever we could get off somewhere by ourselves. When I used to think of telling any of my kin about Pete and me, it was Jack whom I thought about telling. I was glad I hadn't.

I was, if not the oddity that day, the focal point of the proceedings, the one with whom everybody wanted to have a word. For me, it was as though the whole thing was being done in my honor. For them, I was the excuse for this wonderful thing; they had not kept the graves of their departed, but today they were changing their ways. They would call me over to see a stone they had cleaned or a grave weeded and raked. Sometimes, it was even as though they were preparing a place for me there.

When we had finished our food we went back to work. And we worked in a satisfied way, a way with no toil in it, like the sentimental paintings of happy laborers you see in the lobbies of government buildings. All but Uncle Fate, who took the hard jobs of digging up the roots of the burned saplings and setting up the stones that had fallen over. While the rest of us raked and hoed and carried off debris, he set the fence to right, straightening out bent palings and getting the gate to work again. While we were talking about planting boxwood, he got his chain saw out of the back of his truck, filled it with gasoline and started toward the cedar tree that had grown into the fence. I persuaded him not to cut the tree down, but my argument in favor of the beauty of the cedar and its age and charm put a sneer on his face which stayed there the rest of the day as if he'd had a stroke. Through his curled lips he spoke the only two sentences that he was to speak to me that day. The first, a question, "You got a girl up there in New York?" and when I answered no, the second, a simple statement meant to put me in the place he thought I should be, "Me and Fan been planning to do this ourselves, anyway."

Daddy was there that day and acting happy in the way he does when he is happy, which is grinning and talking the legs off everybody. That day he did not pretend that he wasn't pleased with what was going on. And he did not pretend that he wasn't pleased with me. He told anybody that would listen, even the ones who already knew, that I was the one they should thank. No matter to him that all I had done was to think up the idea and set the day. When he had talked everybody else to death he took me around to many of the graves and told me about the people buried there. He showed me the graves of his father and mother. His eyes teared up as he talked of his father, whom he called Diddy. He told of how hard Diddy made him work. He said how much he had hated farm work.

"Diddy tried to get them to let my brother off from the war, 'cause my brother knew how to farm," he said, as we stood over his brother's grave. Nothing he said was what I thought to be complimentary or warm, but it was the tone in his voice as he listed his father's faults, the drinking, the temper. That quiet voice of my daddy, low-pitched and almost sweetly toned, was a voice in him which I had never heard before and have not since. I am glad I remember it. It was the voice of one who has to love the bad things in a person or nothing at all. I'll never love anything like that.

About his mother he said very little, except that once she had left for a whole week during the thick of tobacco harvesting time. Strolled off down the road one day just before dark, he said. She came back as calmly as she had left, put her suitcase down on the back porch, took her apron from the nail on the kitchen door where she had left it, tied it around her waist and made supper. They asked her once and only once where she had been.

" 'Somewhere better than this place, and I didn't like it,' she said," my daddy told me. "And we knew not to ask again. The only difference we saw was that from then on she worked only as much as she wanted to and not as much as we needed her to."

He showed me the grave of his baby sister, who had died of pneumonia at the age of three and was buried in one corner under a small stone with a lamb carved on the top. He told me how he had laid the tiny casket on the backseat of his Chevrolet coupe and driven it to the graveyard himself. As he told of his little sister, dead and buried, his lifelong fear of pneumonia made sense to me. I knew finally. It was simple why he used almost to threaten me with it as if the disease were his to inflict like a switch or his belt. Understood why he would say, "You're going to catch pneumonia, and when you do I'm going to whip you," when he caught me going barefoot before the first of May or without a coat in winter. It was a revelation, logical as a riddle answered after years of wondering and resentment over mysterious unfairnesses and arbitrary prohibitions. Watching him and listening to him that day, I wanted to forgive him for a while, or at least I thought I did. Remembering it now, I could almost be his son. I could try again, face him and forget that shotgun. But that small window to the attic of my heart did not remain unshuttered long after that day we cleaned off this graveyard. And now, thinking about him and what he had to tell me that day reminds me of other things I almost forgave, but did not. Do not.

I nail the window shut against a chill on a summer night and the smell of horsehair upholstery. It was the chill of the summer night's air all green and wet coming through the opened front window of his car. That chill he did not try to protect me from. There was a girl, all young, and yellow from the lights of the dashboard. I stood behind the front seat and watched the beams from the headlights lead us down the curvy black road where a man had been killed doing what we were doing. The high summer growth on both sides of the road, green and gray in the headlit night, peeling away as we sped faster and faster, and Daddy swerving into the other lane then, to show the girl how it had happened, jerking the steering wheel back and the car, under his control, straightening up where it was supposed to be and Daddy, with one finger, slowly rotating the steering wheel off to the right and the car veering onto the edge of the ditch bank. And her saying, "Quit, now. Quit it." And I, worried for her, told her nothing would happen. I remember saying he was just showing us what the man had done. "We are not going to have a wreck and die," I remember saying. "He is just showing us," I said.

Daddy stood over his little sister's grave and cried and said how pretty she had been. He called her name.

In the car that night he told me to sit down in the backseat, and I did, and the girl slipped over in the front seat until her head was where mine had been. I moved over by the door so I could look where we were going. We raced along the side of the road until we came to the place where the man had gone into the ditch, and the place was still there, the weeds and bushes torn away and the mud smoothed out like cake icing.

"You trying to scare me to death?" the girl said. We had stopped by the side of the cricket-noisy road.

"I wasn't scared," I remember saying. And Daddy turned around, and by the dashboard lights which moved over to one side of his face, I saw half a grin on his mouth and a dark, wet curl on his forehead, and then he laughed at me like I have since heard men laugh at me in the dark. So many of them had wet curls on their foreheads.

"You won't scared, were you?" Daddy said. And I answered, "No," just as I have answered the others. I laughed. Then Daddy looked at the girl and his grin went away. "You move back over there," he said to her. "Not now. Later," he said.

We drove home, and pulled into the front yard, and Daddy reached his arm up over the backseat and opened the car door for me. I got out and started walking to the front steps.

"Tell Mama I'll be back before long," I remember hearing him say. And when I turned around to say I would, the girl was back close to him. He put his arm around her. He had

HOME FOR THE DAY

to so he could back the car out of the driveway. I went into the house and told Mama what Daddy had told me to tell her. She sat down, and I crawled into her lap, and she read two Bible stories to me and then put me to bed.

All that I nearly forgave that day here in this very graveyard standing just a few feet from where I am now with my daddy telling about his baby sister as the smoke from Uncle Fate's fire swirled up into the spring sky. And now, here over the grave of someone who was dear to me, I remember something else about that night, something else I will have to forgive or not. Perhaps it is not something about that night in particular that I remember and will or will not forgive, but maybe it is something about other nights like it. Was it the night of the young, yellow girl and the Bible stories that I remember waking in the dark to the sound of my mother's voice in another room?

"Don't, Carleton. Don't," quietly hissing, but as urgent as a scream, and then, not from her, a sharp sound like a stick breaking, and a thud. Then a yelp halfway in her throat, not allowed out of her mouth but lodged there like some nasty medicine that won't go down.

Or was it some other night or that night when later her voice and the smell of my daddy were in the room with me, at the foot of my bed? And did I, on that night of the country road and the place where a man had run his car in the ditch and gotten killed and my mother's voice was in the room before I woke up and then after, pretend not to wake up, did not even open my eyes, did not even move or vary my waking breathing from my sleep breath because the yellow girl had been in the car and my daddy had told me to tell Mother what I told her? Was it that night, as I lay there feigning sleep like a cornered animal will feign death, that I heard my mother say to the smell, "If you can leave him, then go." I remember those words and that smell and the sound of her voice. Then it was quiet and the smell was gone and I opened my eyes and saw the foot of the bed where the voice and the smell had been and there was only the light from the street lamp there. And the sounds were again outside my room, back where they slept, strangled sounds, smothered yelps and barks, worse because these sounds responded one to the other in a twisted harmony. I was alone. It was as if they had moved away together and left me behind.

But I cannot remember now, here in this graveyard by the grave of what was mine, and not far from the grave of my daddy's little sister, whether the night of the young, yellow girl, and the wind through the car window, and the one story from the Bible of Zaccheus and the sycamore tree and the other of the wedding at Canaan, whether that night was the same night that my daddy could not leave me.

Anything I can remember, I will not forgive.

Not knowing what Pete wanted, I took a guess that it would be my lies. Daddy, I made out, was an educated Democrat of the Progressive South who had studied law but had declined to take the bar examinations, deciding instead to write poetry. "Bad," I would say with a sad smile. In addition to his main occupation of poetry, I invented as his avocation the pursuit of an elected position in the state legislature. "Never won a single contest, poor fellow. Too liberal, alas." All this I made possible for him by endowing the family with substantial tobacco land, completely entailed. I told Pete that I had been born in the family home, Maple Knoll, which was an architectural mishmash, the kitchen being pre-Revolutionary and the main house antebellum Greek Revival with a modernization in 1870 to Victorian in the Queen Anne style. The bed on which I was born was the ceremonial birthing bed of my ancestors—a simple head- and footboard made by my great-great-great-great-grandfather who had come here in 1779 from the Virginia Tidewater. The bed was made from pine wood that he had cut himself from the forest on his new property. In my head, the forest was where this graveyard is now. That made-up detail pleased me endlessly, nurtured my overdeveloped sense of the dramatically appropriate, and no one ever questioned why my ancestor would see to a bed and the beginnings of a graveyard before he set himself to the task of insuring the means of life. No one asked why he did not first clear a field. I, of course, had thought of his lack of consideration for the practical, or rather the inconsistency in my tale, and was ready. "What has made my family has also undone it. That is, our tendency to perform the symbolic act before taking the practical action" is what I would have said.

It was to pay homage to their ancestors and to remind themselves and the whole family of its simple beginnings that the ladies of the family had, at the onset of labor, forsworn their comfortable *boudoirs* in favor of this rough but venerated cot which sat in a little jump connecting the old kitchen to the main house.

How Pete loved that lie. After I told it to him, he made me tell it to everybody.

"Tell them about Maple Knoll," he would say. "Tell them about the bed."

Anything Pete loved I wanted him to have. I told that lie every time he asked me to tell it. And the more I told it the better it got, better in the sense of further from the truth. The more I lied the more he loved me.

Pete was worth lying for. The first time I ever saw him was in an airport. We were going to the same place, both hired for the same summer theater in a stupid little town in Illinois. I could not tell from the first time I saw him that he was worth lying for. It took some time for me to start wanting him that badly. But he was tall and blond and handsome in a way that included sex as an afterthought, like a pale blue seersucker suit or a cream-colored foreign car, very sporty, sitting still and all trimmed with chrome.

I was with somebody at the time. This two-year thing with a fellow named Dorsey. Dorsey was sure enough of his looks to pull off his name, but was lacking in self-regard sufficient to the extent that he thought I was the best he could do. He had said from the start, however, that he loved me. I believed him and stayed with him because it was New York City, and I was poor and had to share a bed with somebody. I had come to the slovenly conclusion that if I could not be under a roof with someone I loved, I would have a roof over my head under which I was loved. I told myself this to keep from having to tell myself how it really was. Dorsey had a rent-controlled apartment. More precisely, he had an illegal sublet of a rent-controlled apartment. We split one hundred dollars a month for one room on Barrow Street. For that, I had to sit tight until something better came along. The bottom line was green.

But when I saw Pete sit down across from me at the airport that day I, like my bogus ancestor, did not think of what I needed. What I wanted and all I wanted was that handsome-as-I-needed-him-to-be fellow. When I saw Pete I quit sitting tight and started to consider what it would be like to sleep in the same bed as he. What happened next amazed me as much as when what you want is what you get and it is what you ought to have. He smiled at me. Help my life! When he smiled you couldn't tell if he was pretty or friendly. God, he was so pretty it made him friendly. Or maybe the other way. I don't know. I just know that nothing else is like Pete smiling, and nothing else will do. He smiled a lot, nearly all the time. It had such vigor, that smile, as though he had been given the responsibility to keep the world welcomed. The smile was generous, as generous as Pete turned out to be. That smile was Pete's work. And before long, I came to make that smile my work. Watching it, guarding it and sometimes making it go away just so I could bring it back were the tasks of my calling.

I knew that I was not good enough for Pete and that to get him would not be easy for me. He was like everything else that is fine. I had not stopped measuring myself against fine things—my grandmother's china and silver and furniture. I don't know why I did what I did. Instead of just staring at Pete as I wanted to, I took hope and tried to think of reasons why he should try to like me. To keep from looking at him too much I made a list of all the beautiful things I had read about or heard of which were in the care of people who were, in terms of beauty, or intelligence, or honesty, of less than high quality themselves. I thought of great paintings in the palaces of dictators, of murderers whose constant wives move near the prisons in which their husbands are confined, of the talents which can be possessed by sons of bitches. I thought of my daddy with my mother, and me eating off my grandmother's china, and for a minute I lost hope, but then I thought of things that I had wanted and had not gotten. I rationalized that Pete was my due. For though I was never as fine as anything I desired, I had hope that fine people don't measure themselves against those who desire them. They are possessed, I told myself then, of a certain magnanimity, or perhaps inherent perfection creates carelessness and a lack of selectivity. I twisted logic, mused simplistically, and settled for that as truth. I plowed mud.

I don't remember who spoke first or what we said. I just

remember that at some time during the talk which got us acquainted I noticed him getting finer and farther away, and I didn't know what to do except ask him straight out if he was like other fine things. Later, during the years we were together and we would remember that day, he claimed that he did not understand half the time what I was talking about. Well, that showed intelligence. He would say that he thought I was the type who had to talk about what he called dull, deep things before getting down to business. But I knew what trouble having to hope is, and I wanted to save myself that if I could. He thought I was flirting, but I don't think there was more than a wilted bit of flirtation in the way I asked him what I did.

"Do you think that perfection wants and deserves perfection?" I asked Pete, out of the clear blue of my hope.

He was looking at the television monitor which displayed flight information. He gazed up at the screen with its lists of acronyms and numbers and departure times with a look of delight as though he were watching fireworks.

"I sure hope not," he said. "If it does, will you still sit with me on the plane?" He picked up a small valise that had been at his feet, turned away from me and headed toward the door that led to the airplane. The stewardess took his ticket and looked up at him, and I know he must have smiled at her because she just lit up in a way that was not professional. I saw as well the shifting of skin on the back of Pete's head that would be from then on how I could see his smile whether it was cast toward me or away. I smiled too and felt the back of my head to see if it would do the same thing Pete's had done. I was grinning like a fool with my hand on the back of my head when Pete turned in the doorway.

"Look," he said, "I don't believe in stuff like perfection. Sit with me."

On the plane, I talked about myself. I made up my story as I went along. I watched Pete's face, and it told me what to tell. Some of it I had made up over the years. I told him lies I had told myself, and his face, bright and amazed, told me that I had not invented anything I could not believe. My lies worked. The truth I knew the effect of, and it was an effect which I did not wish to achieve. So I did not speak a word of truth. The lies which before I had crafted on the basis of feasibility were now constructed to seduce. They had a purpose. Through the years the important truths came out. He'd figure them out—ask again and again the specifics in a way that made it clear to me that he knew I'd been lying. I'd come clean, and he'd just laugh and say how enchanting it was to have been loved right off as much as that. The trivial lies, the ones he delighted in most, I let him die believing. Or he died letting me think he believed them.

I<small>T'S AN UNTIDY BUSINESS</small> how my life comes to me here in this graveyard. I want to remember Pete and how I got him, but I cannot hold my mind.

It is the day set aside for the county schoolchildren to go to the fair. We got out of school early today. Twelve o'clock. Any other day I would be disappointed. I like school. I am made a big deal of there because I am smart. Last year, in the sixth grade, I scored tenth-grade-plus on every subject except arithmetic. On that I scored sixth grade, which didn't surprise me since arithmetic is unfair in that it abides only by its own rules. I could not even spell the word correctly until I learned the trick of "A rat in Tom's house might eat Tom's ice cream."

None of us is supposed to know what any of the others of us made on the test, but as the teacher was grading them she looked up from her work and told us something we were not supposed to know.

"Class," she said, "I have just graded the test of a student who scored ten tenth-grade-pluses."

I looked around, but I did not see anybody who I thought could have done it. I did not think it could have been me, and I had nothing but ill will toward my classmates and knew that none of them could have done something I could not have done, or that if one of them had, it had been luck or cheating.

But again, this business of remembering is untidy. I was the one who made the unprecedented score on the test, which the teacher, Mrs. Eatmon, showed me by having me sit beside her and pointing to the blocks on the scoring sheet beside my name. I watched as the lead point of her pencil paused at each block indicating the subject, and I watched as the pencil point moved to a small square inset in the subject blocks and tapped ten tenth-grade pluses.

I have to pull my mind to how I got out of school early and ran home to go to the fair. And how we did not go as we were supposed to go.

The first thing I want to see when I get home is my daddy's car. I hate that redneck car of his. It is a black '61 Ford that he has fixed so he can break every speed limit and outrun the highway patrol. He has gone so far as to paint a red streak down the side of it. He has put decals on it to make it look like fire is coming out of the front wheel wells. When my mother and I drive to church in it, as we have to do, having no other way to go, I think it looks as if we're taking Satan to the Branch Creek Methodist Church in a car that has been custom-made for him. We have to park the thing right out front in the spot reserved for the choir director, who is my mother. I don't think she has any desire to serve, but she is the best singer in the congregation, and she's had some piano lessons. She never has said she doesn't want to be choir director. But the preacher asked over and over before she agreed. She didn't say anything, until she said yes. She'd just smile and look down. But then a morning came when we were trying to sneak away in the car after services. We had parked way down the street, but Miss Hyland, whose money built the church, was walking home that day for some unlucky reason, and just as she got alongside of us, she tilted her head to one side, smiled as if she had eaten a green persimmon and said to my mother, "Amy, honey, that is the sportiest car I've ever seen."

Mother called the preacher when we got home and told him she'd prayed about it, and she thought she ought to serve. What it looked like to me was that she decided to do it because it makes up for the car we have to drive to church, which is the car I want to see in the driveway of the straight house today, the day of the fair.

But first I am running home every step of the way, as all of us are who live in the town and don't have to ride the school bus. We are a pack of fair-hungry dogs and we run and leap over nothing because often we just have to leap. Johnny Ray is out front, and I am right behind him. He is the fastest runner in the seventh grade because he is supposed to be in the ninth. I am the second-fastest because I am a smart sissy and have had to learn how to run fast. Johnny is the only friend I have. He knows this as well as I do, but it doesn't matter to him. He is as good a friend as he would be if I had a thousand friends and he was my best. He will get to the eighth grade with me if I have anything to do with it, and I do. I have been doing two copies of all the homework this year, one perfect, which I turn in with my name on it and one with enough mistakes to have been done by Johnny but still correct enough to earn a passing grade. Mrs. Eagles is pleased with Johnny's progress.

"Not because it is perfect, Johnny," she says when she praises his homework, "far from it. But it is good for you and shows what you are capable of when you set your mind to it."

Johnny is a real man. He is never impressed by anybody, but is the one everybody tries to impress. What teachers think of him or what they tell him to do means nothing to Johnny. Earlier this year Mrs. Eagles made a talk about cigarettes and how we should not smoke. As soon as she left the classroom for a moment, Johnny got up from his desk, walked up to the front of the room and from Mrs. Eagles' purse took out a pack of Winstons. He held the pack high over his head for all of us to see. Then he took three cigarettes for himself and went back to his desk. The other students pretend to like him well, because they know it would be dangerous for them if he thought they didn't. By me he is loved. As tough as he is it does not seem to bother him that I am a sissy. There are many who picked on me before we caught up to Johnny in the seventh grade. They would like to pick on me still, but when they try, Johnny is there before they see him coming. "Leave him alone," he will say to anybody who teases me or hits me. To me, there is nothing more beautiful to hear. The boys are respectful of him. They move away if he wants to make a game of marbles where they have been playing. They never talk about doing it and playing with themselves around him, for they know that they don't know what they're talking about, and they know Johnny knows how wrong they've got it. The girls claim they are afraid of him.

"Well, you can just see everything he's got," I heard one of them say to her friend.

HOME FOR THE DAY

On the playground, when the weather is too hot for him, he takes off his shirt. Some teacher always makes him put it back on. Then when she turns her back, he pulls his shirt up and grabs his nipples and makes like he's squirting something at her. It's the funniest thing I've ever seen in my life. None of the rest of us boys ever takes off his shirt, for those of us who are not fat are skinny. In the shower after gym class his body is the bottom of a brook. It is all like water over smooth stones and rippled sand. The elastic in the legs of his underwear has lost its courage. In the locker room, when he sits down to put on his trousers, everything spills out. I watch, and he sees me watching and says that he is too damn big, and he just laughs. I want to laugh too, but I can't make a sound. It's like I'm falling, what happens in my belly when I see him like that.

He'll just stay home on days the rest of us wouldn't miss for the world. These include Valentine's Day, when we make and exchange red paper hearts which we trim with paper doilies and such mess as that, the day we have our pictures made, any day of a pep rally and the day before we get out for Christmas, when we go down to the library and make presents for our teachers. It is because of Johnny that we make and do not buy presents for our teachers. In the past, before I started school, I have been told that to bring a small gift for the teacher was not only thought to be a nice gesture but was pretty much expected. These were never expensive gifts, simple little things from Woolworth's mostly, face powder, brush and comb sets, sachets. Now that is something I'd like to do, go shopping at Woolworth's. I can't make a thing that anybody would want for Christmas with construction paper and dried macaroni. Last Christmas I pestered Mother to let me buy something until she called my teacher, Mrs. Eagles, to find out if it would be all right. She blabbed the reason why it wouldn't to Mother. The story is that when Johnny was in the first grade he presented his teacher with a package he had wrapped himself in green construction paper which he had taken from the supply closet. When the teacher opened the present she held up the plate that Johnny had given to her, thanked him, then put it away with the other gifts. The next Christmas, it was announced that students were not to buy presents for their teachers, but that they would be given an opportunity to make a nice gift during school hours. It was just that the plate Johnny had given the teacher was discovered to have a tiny bit of dried egg on the rim. Johnny's father came to get the plate sometime during the holidays.

I wish I didn't know this, or could stay home too.

Johnny skips school as well on the first day back from Christmas, when we get up and tell what we got. I figure it's because he doesn't get much to speak of. When he is absent is the only time the others make fun of him, and I wish I thought it was droll, but I don't. What I do wish is that I was big and tough and rich, because then I could kill anybody who was crazy enough to make fun of Johnny if I was around, and I could buy for him the thing he wants most in the world, which is a '57 Chevrolet. He is not old enough to drive yet, but will be in a year old enough for a learner's permit, which he does not need for he already knows *how* to drive. None of us has ever seen him drive. He just says he can. I am the only one who believes him. Johnny picked a guy in the ninth grade up by the seat of his pants and flung him to the ground because he said he didn't believe Johnny could drive.

HOME FOR THE DAY

"I don't give a fuck whether you think I can drive or not," Johnny said. "But I'm kicking your ass for calling me a liar." Johnny says that word when he's mad. Not a-s-s, the other one, and when he says it, it comes out low and short like a hiccough. Usually, that word is a word I don't like to hear, but when Johnny uses it, how he uses it is what it's for. If he has his shirt off when he says it, I can see his stomach muscles playing with him.

He has none of the things which I take for granted, like a dollar a week, a Sunday suit and pair of shoes, birthday cakes, a record player. But he has other things which I wish were mine: high-topped tennis shoes, a folding pocket knife which he can nonetheless throw and make stick in a tree without the blade collapsing, and a secondhand bicycle which has been made sturdy and fine in his care. There is nothing fancy about it. It has no hand grips or chain guard, but it is fast and dependable. He does not ride it to school because he doesn't want to leave it outside unattended the whole day. Of course he is the only one who has ridden it since it came to him. I think he stole it, but he says that somebody his daddy does yardwork for gave it as payment.

Finally, there is his wallet, which never has more than a quarter in it but contains things that I don't even know how to want or where to buy, if I did. In the place where he would keep folding money if he had any, he keeps an unwrapped rubber and a three of hearts with a picture on the back of just the privates of a colored man and the privates of a white woman somehow hooked together. This picture broke my mind the first time he showed it to me. I stared for a long time at each part of the picture. In my mind, I separated the white part from the black part, and in my way, using what little knowledge I had picked up about private parts other than my own, made sense of the two things, black and white, for myself. I see the picture from time to time. What happens is that I will have to see the picture. He will show it to me, and then I will get disgusted for a long time until I have to see it again. Always, I understand the parts, but I never can understand how they link. It breaks my mind.

"Why do they do that?" I ask Johnny.

"Because it feels good," he answers. But what he says does not explain it.

AS WE HIT THE AVENUE, where my grandmother lives, Johnny and I are still out front. I hear only a few of the other boys running behind us now. Most of them peeled off a ways back. They live closer to the school than Johnny and I. They're probably home by now. We see a car pass loaded with some of those who take the bus home. They are already on their way, and this kills me, so I run faster and for the first time ever I am running side by side with Johnny. He turns toward me and chassés along without losing ground. We are almost to my street. Another car passes loaded with people I know. The windows are down, and we hear them laughing and yelling inside. Some of them see us, but they do not wave. They think I don't know where they are going, and they don't want to let me know. They intend to use up the fair before Johnny and I can get to it.

I am so mad with them that I pass my street.

"Johnny, too far!" I holler, and I stop and begin to lope backwards. I watch him pull the distance between us. "Too far."

He does not turn around but yells to me over his shoulder. "Got to go home first," he says. "Got to get my money."

This is it. I thought we had worked this out. I get five dollars from my daddy, and Johnny has been thinking probably that he can get as much as two-fifty from his. That gives us three-seventy-five each. Not enough, but it's better for him. He was supposed to bring the money with him and come home with me. We are losing time. We are passed by a church bus, loaded down. It seems hopeless, but I am not ready to go without Johnny.

"Don't come back. We'll pick you up." I know Daddy will not want to do this, go out of the way. Something that small can make Daddy turn hard. But I make my plan as I run along. Maybe if I tune up and cry. I get in Mother's lap and we just look pitiful. Sometimes something just as small as the thing which hardened him can fix him. Sometimes. It will all take time, though.

Johnny moves out, and I turn around and run faster than I thought I could. A few quick strides and I am back at the turnoff. The dirt street is straight from here to the straight house where I live. It is the last house on the street, and I tick off the distance, the sound of my running feet bouncing back to me off the brick veneer fronts of the other straight houses on the street, the space between each house a silence that I try to make shorter and shorter by running faster. I cannot see my daddy's house yet, but my mind runs ahead of my feet. What I will see will be that despised car and maybe Daddy leaning up against it waiting for me, or maybe he will have the hood up checking the oil, or maybe he will be polishing some of the chrome or down on his knees examining the car for scratches. If he is doing any of these things, I will want to know why he just didn't come and pick Johnny and me up at the school. But I won't ask. No time. Not enough time for that. What if he's washing the thing?

The street is quiet. Not like any ordinary day when school is let out. There are no games going on and bicycles are lying where they were dropped. The only car in any of the driveways is where the Goodwins live, except for my daddy's car, which I believe is there although I can't see it yet.

The Goodwins are Pentecostal and can't go to the fair. Earl Goodwin is sitting on the front stoop of the house bouncing a basketball on the step below and looking like he wishes he were Methodist. I don't have time to say hey or even wave to him.

I am halfway up the street and the bush that Mother planted at the driveway comes into view. I knock off the houses. Lucas', and a few more feet of Daddy's driveway pushes out toward the street. Moores', Taylors', and I can see the lamppost tangled with dead ivy. Skinners', and now I should see the red-bullet tail-lights of my daddy's car.

I don't see the car. It's under the carport, then. I won't look. I run with my head down, watching my feet spin the dirt street away behind me. This way, when I am standing in the driveway, and I look up, the car will be there. Maybe I can find something to like about the thing. But I can't wait, and anyway, I am at the edge of Daddy's lot. I recognize the grass.

The car is not there. Under the carport is what is always under the carport: the lawn mower and a two-gallon tin of gasoline, a hoe, a flowerpot with wires for hanging and nothing in it but dried dirt and a depression in the center where something tried to grow and didn't, and my bicycle, which I never ride because it is green. The only sign of my daddy's car is an oil spot on the cement, and it is not wet and glistening. The last place I try is the back of the house, where there is an outdoor spigot. If there is such a thing as luck, he will be washing that hateful contraption.

There is no such thing as luck. I go into the house, and in the kitchen, Mother is on the telephone. When she sees me she turns her back and curls herself around the receiver. I sit down at the kitchen table, and wait for her to look at me. I will make her see my face. It is not her fault that my daddy is not here, but it is not my fault either. I can't fix it. She has to. She is trying. Everything she says into the receiver, she says twice, once softly so I won't hear and then she repeats what she has said, raising her voice so the person on the other end can hear her. I hear the echo before the source.

"Red? Is this Red?" She is calling the place where she knows she will find my daddy. It is the place my grandmother calls *that place your daddy can't pass by.* It is really called Berenice's. The place is on the highway to the county seat. I pass by it often. I will never go in it. It is where Daddy drinks. It is a place that has a lot of cars out front, especially at night, and they are cars that are the kind I don't like.

"Red, this is Amy. Is Carleton there?" There is a pause, and Mother turns and looks at me, and I look back and try to make my face say that she has to fix this. "Red, I know he *is.*" She waits again, and I go over to her and put the top of my head on her belly. "Tell him I don't want anything," she says, and I can feel her say it. I hear her hang up the telephone, and I can feel her start to cry, and now I don't want her to have to fix it anymore, but she lifts my head up, and takes my hand, and we go up and down the street from house to house to see if there is anybody who will give me a ride to the fair.

"We have to get a ride for Johnny, too," I say after we give up knocking on the Skinners' front door. But Mother doesn't say anything. I let it go. It's useless. Everybody has gone who is going. I do not tell Mother this, though. I let her keep trying. I stand in the yard as she goes up the front steps of Moores', Taylors', and I watch her try. I watch her cup her hand up to the dark windows in the front doors and look into other people's houses to see if they are home. I watch her pound the doors until her knuckles are red as strawberries. She even tries the Goodwins', though I tell her they won't go near the fair.

"Maybe they are going to a prayer meeting or something and could drop you off," she says as we go around to the back of their house, having had no luck at the front door. Mother bangs on the aluminum door with the heel of her hand, and from inside the house I hear the thump of a basketball coming. Earl Goodwin opens the door holding the ball under his arm. When he sees us he calls, "Ma," and Mrs. Goodwin comes to the door with half her long hair rolled up on top of her head in the way Pentecostals do and the other half down and over one shoulder. She is working the hank of waist-length hair into a braid with both her hands, which pulls her head over to one side as though the hair were caught in the washing machine wringer. She has her mouth full of hairpins. Occasionally, she removes one to fasten a section of the braid around the roll on top. Earl stands behind her steadily bouncing the basketball. She tells him she is going to knock him down if he don't quit it. He quits it, and pushes past her to come outside and stand with me. Mother starts in.

HOME FOR THE DAY

"Lerline, are you taking Earl to the fair this afternoon?" she asks.

Mrs. Goodwin stops working her braid and gets this look on her face like Mother just broke wind. I am afraid she is going to make us all get down on our knees and pray the way she made Earl and me do the time she found us playing gunslingers. Earl and I were under the carport pretending we had stopped off at the saloon for a glass of whiskey—instant iced tea taken from Mrs. Goodwin's kitchen and mixed in a liquor bottle we had found beside the road. When she came out of the house to throw some table scraps into the drainage ditch that runs behind all the houses on the street and saw us pretending to drink whiskey, she dropped the pot she was carrying right in the middle of the carport. It was full of the broth from cooking collard greens mixed with old cornbread. She yanked the bottle out of Earl's hip pocket and threw it up against the side of her house so hard that the iced tea made a big wet star on the brick veneer. She hit Earl in the back of the head and knocked him to his knees. I went down as well, but on my own. It seemed like the thing to do. The three of us prayed on that hard cement for all together a solid half hour. Then Mrs. Goodwin got the Holy Ghost, pretty much forgot about us, and had something that looked like an epileptic fit down there in that puddle of broth and cornbread. That lasted for about fifteen minutes and during it, Earl got up, went to the kitchen and got himself a glass of Kool-Aid, which he was able to finish before the Holy Ghost left and Mrs. Goodwin came back from wherever the Spirit had taken her. Mother and I are Methodist, and I'm not sure what we believe. I don't think we believe in the Holy Ghost, but if we do, we believe that it is in heaven and stays there. But I have been taught to be polite. I knelt with Mrs. Goodwin through it all. I even shook a little bit with her just to be nice. That is why I think she does not say what she probably would like to say to Mother.

"We don't believe in the fair," she says instead. "Me and Earl is going to prayer meeting. What don't you and him come with us?"

"I OUGHT TO HAVE known better," Mother says as we are walking back home. "Anytime you ask her for help you have to pay for it. Twice. Once with the invitation to church, and once with having to think up an excuse for not going, and as far as she is concerned, there are no excuses."

"Ours wasn't very good," I say.

"She thinks I'm hell-bound in the first place because I sell Avon," says Mother.

Mother had told Mrs. Goodwin that we couldn't go to prayer meeting because I had my heart set on the fair. Mrs. Goodwin said she had her heart set on Jesus. "And Earl does too," she said. "Don't you, sugar?"

"Yeah, I reckon so," Earl said. His mama tried to smile at him, but she lost some of the hairpins she was holding in her mouth and had to tighten her lips again.

"But couldn't you just drop him and his little friend off on your way?" Mother asked.

"We don't even go by the place," said Mrs. Goodwin, losing the rest of the hairpins. "We go the long way around to keep from having to pass by all that sin." She was still holding on to different parts of her hairdo, so she shut the door in our faces with her elbow.

We go back home, but we haven't given up yet. Mother goes to the phone to call Berenice's again, but first has to run somebody off the line.

"Bessie, I need this line for my child," she says into the receiver. "Don't think that'll run her off," she says to me. When she gets through to Berenice's this time, she asks Red to ask Daddy doesn't he care a thing for his little boy. Me. She has tried this before when this kind of thing happens, but I don't think Red ever asks him, for if he did, I just feel like Daddy would come home.

"Bessie, if you're listening why don't you try to help and bring your fine automobile over here and take my child and his friend to the fair," Mother says, just before she flicks the plunger to get another dial tone. "That got her off, but not before she knows every bit of our business." Mother dials as fast as if the house were on fire. Soon I hear her say, "Mama." She is talking to Grandmother. She asks Grandmother if she can borrow her car to take me to the fair. Then for a while she doesn't say anything. She just listens. When she does speak it is all about something between the two of them. I think she has forgotten about getting me and Johnny to the fair.

"Mama, I don't want to do that," Mother says. "No," she says. "No. No, I'm not going to do that. Will you let me use the car or not?" Mother listens again, then puts the receiver to her chest. "She wants to talk to you," she says, and holds the receiver out to me, and gives me this quick look she has that can make me sit still or move, can make me be quiet or speak up, can make me forget what pleases me and remember what she would like. If I am loving her, the look can make me hate her, and if I am acting like I can't stand her, all she has to do is give me this look that she has, and I will want to hang around her neck. If looks could talk, this one would say, "You have hurt me, and that makes me mad as the devil."

I take the phone anyway. I don't say anything at first. I just look at Mother to see if what I am doing is all right. She is still giving me the look, so it makes me not care if what I am doing is all right. On the other end of the line, I hear a machine running and Grandmother telling the Negro woman what to do.

"Lynn Dora, shut off that thing," Grandmother says, and the machine noise stops. "Do the silver until I'm off the telephone. Honey, wait a minute," she says to me, then back to Lynn Dora, "Huh? Well, yes, but I'm going to use it Sunday."

I hear Lynn Dora say something, but I can't make out what, exactly. Whatever it is irritates Grandmother, for when she speaks again she speaks quickly. She has taken the phone away from her mouth, but I can make out that she knows Lynn Dora can't work on Sunday and that she intends to use the silver on that day and not Lynn Dora. Finally, she gets back to me.

"Sugar, are you there?" she asks.

"Grandmother, I want to go to the fair," I say, and although more than anything I don't want this to happen, my voice starts to wiggle when I say the word fair, and it's like I've got a jawbreaker lodged in my windpipe. "And Johnny, too, Grandmother." Now I'm snuffling, and the words come out of me all jumpy as if I'm being hit on the back every time I say something.

"I know you do, sugar, and Grandmother is going to take

you. Grandmother will take you to the fair every day this week if you want to go, and Johnny, too." That thing in my windpipe comes loose and goes down. I feel like I can talk all I want to. I look over at Mother and try to give her look right back to her. I am not doing it right. It does not change her face. She almost makes me feel bad that I am going to the fair.

"She is going to take me," I say to Mother, and I say this in a way that I hope will make Mother feel awful. She was supposed to fix this. I know she has tried, but I act mean anyway. It is the way she looks at me mostly that makes me do it, but it is just as much that there is meanness in me, I guess. That, and who else is there to blame?

"I sure am going to take you, sugar," Grandmother says. "Did you tell your mama that? And here's what you are going to do for me."

I stop looking at Mother so I can listen better. I want to hear every word of what Grandmother wants me to do, and I am ready to say yes to it all.

"All you have to do is get together all your little things. Tell your mama to pack them up for you. If I take you to the fair, I know you will be so glad and that you will love your sweet grandmother so much that you will want to come live with her, won't you? I know you would rather live here where I am always at home and have a fine car just sitting in the garage all the time ready to take you anywhere you want to go. Ready to take you and Johnny and any of your little friends to the fair every day this week. Why, we can go to fairs all over the state. Wherever there is one in whatever county, why, we will just pick right up and strike out for it."

It sounds like more than a square deal, the way she says it, and I want to do it. I put the phone to my chest the way I have seen Mother do, and I tell her that I have to go live with Grandmother. Mother is over to me so quick I don't see her get there. When I see anything, I see the phone is out of my hand and at her ear. She doesn't listen long before she starts to talk. When she does what she says brings that jawbreaker back up into my windpipe again.

"He will not be going to the fair," Mother says, and puts the phone back on the wall. She gives me the look, and I stop feeling mean and start wanting to be nice to her.

"I can't fix this for you," she says, and the look stops saying the part about being mad and just says what is left. Mother goes over to the sink and gets a paper towel to wipe her eyes with. The phone rings, but Mother does not answer it, and she won't let me. Instead she comes over to the table and sits down. "Come here, baby," she says. I go over and sit on the other side of the table from her. I rub my finger on a sticky spot and roll up whatever it is into a nasty little ball. Things like this nasty place are part of why I wouldn't mind living with Grandmother. We don't have a Negro woman here, and Mother does not always keep things so tidy. I don't think she even sees these spots on the table. She just sees me fidgeting.

"Stop that, baby. I have to talk to you," she says, taking my hand. "You can't go to the fair. Your daddy is not here to take you or to give you the five dollars. I thought I could make a way for you."

This is the first time I have even thought about the money.

"Grandmother will take me," I say, pulling my hand out from under Mother's. I look at her, and I am just me looking at her. I don't try to look mean or nice.

"Do you know what she wants? She wants you and me to

come live with her. That is the only way she will take you. She wants you and me to come, and she wants us to leave Daddy here. You don't want that, do you?"

I don't know if I believe this part. I really think it is just me that Grandmother wants. If she asked Mother it is just because she thinks it would be nice for me.

"Do you want that?" Mother asks. She has to put the paper towel to her eyes again.

"No," I say. "I just want to go to the fair." I go around the table and hang on her neck. She smells like her Avon sample case. Into her ear I whisper, "I don't want to do that really, but we could tell her we would. We could just say we would come and live with her so she would take me to the fair."

Mother pulls me from around her neck, and holds me out in front of her. She smiles, and for a minute I think she thinks it is a good idea. Then her smile slides away, and I can see her thinking.

"But what about this?" she says. "Would we want Daddy to know we had said we would do that?"

"But we wouldn't mean it," I say.

"Even so," she says.

She brings her face close to mine.

She smells like a million flowers.

I am so in love with her.

The phone starts to ring again, but we do not answer it.

WE DIDN'T KNOW it was Daddy who was trying to call us. After a while the phone didn't ring anymore. Mother went to the kitchen and started making something that was supposed to cheer me up. I went outside and sat down on the stoop. Mrs. Goodwin and Earl passed in their

Rambler. She tooted the horn and waved. Earl just stared out the car window at me, and I couldn't tell whether he didn't wave because he knew I was sad or because he was miserable himself. Then it got as quiet as if it were Sunday afternoon.

I thought of Johnny, probably sitting on his front porch wearing a clean undershirt and his best pair of jeans, and I knew I had to walk to his house to let him know that we weren't going. I was going to go inside and tell Mother what I had to do, when I saw him riding up the street on his bicycle, a cigarette in his mouth trailing smoke. His hands were not guiding the bicycle, but were on top of his head like he was sitting under a tree by the creek. He did not have on an undershirt, but was wearing one of his daddy's work shirts. It was unbuttoned all the way and fluttering out behind him just below the trail of cigarette smoke. When he got to the driveway, he did not take his hands off his head to turn but simply leaned in the direction he wanted to go and the bicycle came with him. He rode right up to where I was sitting on the stoop and the front tire of his bicycle kissed the bottom step before he took his feet off the pedals and put his toes on the ground.

"Your daddy ain't here," he said.

"We can't go," I said.

"We're going," he said.

"How can we?" I asked.

He put his cigarette out on the ground, smiled and patted that bar on his bicycle that made it a man's. "I'm taking us," he said.

"We can't. It's ten miles," I said.

He was grinning the way he did whenever he showed me the dirty card. "I been farther than that before," he said.

"I have to tell Mother," I said.

"No, you don't," he said, soft and silky as though he were talking to a kitten or a killer.

"I can't do it," I said.

"You can say I made you," he said. He made it seem as if we were somewhere dark taking our pants down.

I tried to be good. "I'm a good boy," I said.

"No, you ain't," he said. "You're scared is all you are. I'm going. So what are you going to do, be good or see the fair?"

To me, what he said didn't make sense, but it made me want to do it. I went into the house. From the kitchen came the smell of chocolate and the sound of mixing. I stood still in the living room to see if Mother had heard me come into the house.

"What you doing, baby?" I heard her call out to me.

"Nothing," I said. I went to her bedroom. On her dresser was the black case with *Avon* printed in gold letters on the flap. I opened the case and saw myself in the mirror attached to the inside of the lid. I could see that Johnny was right about me. I did not look like a good boy, and I was scared.

Lipstick samples like gold bullets were displayed in a little ammunition belt attached to the inside of the case. Behind was a pocket with a ten-dollar bill and four ones. I took the ten. Then I patted on some of the cologne that was in there. I hoped Johnny wouldn't know that it was for women, but I hoped he'd like it. I closed the case and left the room. I crept through the house and had my hand on the front doorknob when Mother called my name. I did not answer. She did not call me again or come to find me, so I went back outside and hopped sideways onto the crossbar of Johnny's bicycle.

"Slide back towards me," Johnny said. "It's easier if we're both close together, and don't it feel good," he said, chuckling low down in his throat. I did what he told me to do, and he stood up on the pedals and pumped us out of the yard and into the street. We were going faster together on Johnny's bicycle than I had ever gone on the ugly green thing of mine alone. I was moving, and I was not having to try to move. If it was hard pedaling for Johnny, I couldn't tell.

We rushed into and away from everything so fast that the street and houses and trees of the town seemed to split and peel away behind us, and then were not there, for when I turned to look back to see where we were coming from, there was only Johnny's bare chest and tight-skinned stomach and his strong legs pushing me forward into the windy world. Soon we got to the edge of town and were past everything that I had ever ridden by on a bicycle. I had traveled the highway to the city in my daddy's car often, so many times that I had stopped noticing what was on it, but on my ride with Johnny the farmhouses and woods showed themselves to me again. The highway was lighter colored than the black streets of Branch Creek, and as we traveled down it, sparkles of light appeared always just in front of us. The countryside and even the broken bottles and scraps of paper by the side of the road, which had always whizzed by me before, lay still as they are supposed to do, and Johnny and I moved past them as though on parade.

We rode that bicycle every way. We laughed. We changed positions without stopping, like trick riders. When my backside got sore from sitting on the bar, Johnny, holding the handlebars, vaulted up and over me, and I somehow squirmed under him and onto the seat. He stood up in front of me and pedaled, and I could turn around then and see from where we had come, but by then it was a new place with no connection to what I knew to be the start. There was only as far as he could see in front of him and as far as I could see behind. I watched his hips go up and down like pistons, taking us closer to the fair. For a while, I sat on the carrier over the rear wheel and held on to his waist, then we switched, and he sat back there, his arms stretched out to grip the handlebars, and hugging me to him. Then we twisted around until we were back to the first way with me sitting on the crossbar. He would be all around me again, pressing against my back, and I could smell the cigarettes on his breath. I rode on the handlebars facing into the wind for a while and then backwards facing Johnny just looking at him and laughing. He told me to take a cigarette out of his pocket and put it into his mouth and light it for him, and I did, and we never even slowed down. The wind would hit my back and swirl in between us, and we could smell cigarettes and sweat from Johnny and cologne from me.

"You smell like a girl," Johnny said, smiling.

"I know," I said, and I smiled, too. And when he saw that I didn't care, he didn't care either, and he would press closer to me. Sometimes his nose would be in my hair, and his breath would be like warm water all over my head, and that felt good, as if it was what ought to be even though I knew it was something that God saw wherever it happened, and remembered and sent to hell not everybody it happened to, but everybody who liked it.

We came to where the viaduct humps high over the railroad tracks, and we had to get off and walk the bicycle up. At the top, I told him I wanted him to sit on the bar and let me guide the bicycle down, and he did. We went down so fast that the frame started to shake. When the hill ran out, and the going got hard again, Johnny took over, telling me that coming down the hill with me guiding the bicycle had been fun, but that he would rather pedal than have me carry him, and that was how I wanted it anyway. So he stood up on the pedals again and kept us going, and he started to rub against me more often and since I smelled like a girl it didn't bother him that he didn't stop himself. I looked up over my shoulder at him, and all sorts of things that I didn't say came into my head.

"Turn around, sugar, and hold on," he said.

"Okay, baby," I said. Johnny sat back down on the seat, and I didn't feel him against me anymore. When I looked back to see why, he was staring straight at the road ahead, and he looked hard, far off, as if what he was doing was work and he was going somewhere he didn't want to go and having to carry someone he didn't want to have to carry.

"You don't say stuff like that," he said. He didn't look at me when he said it, and I knew I had messed it up, and for a while I was what I was, and he was what he was, and every time I smelled myself I wanted to wash. It stayed like that for a long time. Just going with all the fun out of it. We had to stop for Johnny to rest, and sitting by the side of the road under a tree full of diseased and stunted apples I asked to see the playing card, hoping that it might make him forget that I had called him baby. He took the card out of his wallet and flipped it through the air toward me. I tried to talk about the picture with Johnny. I said, "Wowee!" and "Hot Dog!" and I rubbed the picture against my zipper, but Johnny just sat there tossing rotten apples into the road and not saying anything.

"He sure looks like he is having fun," I said, talking about what to me looked like the he part of the picture. Johnny stopped throwing apples and looked at me and laughed so hard that he started coughing, and he fell back on the ground still laughing and rolled over to where I was and pushed me down, and I started laughing, too.

"What are we laughing at?" I asked.

"At you," he said. "At what you said."

So I said it again. "Boy, he sure does look like he is having a good old time." Johnny whooped so loud that the birds in the apple tree scattered like buckshot into the air, and then he jumped on me.

"He?" Johnny said, poking my ribs. "He? There ain't no he in that picture."

"I know. You know what I mean," I said, squirming and giggling.

"You don't even know, do you? It's two gals in that picture. The man part is artificial." Johnny snatched the card from me, got up and put it back into his wallet. I didn't know what he was talking about, but I was glad I didn't know if that could make him laugh.

"How can it be two gals?" I asked.

"Don't worry about it, sugar. Let's go," he said.

"Okay, Johnny," I said, and soon he was pressing against me and calling me sugar every time he called me anything.

We were getting close to Berenice's, and we could hear music, just a tuneless whine at first whenever the wind was right, then bits of a sad melody as we got closer, then words to a song which Johnny recognized and started to sing.

"I fall to pieces, whoa, whoa, whoa," he sang, and bumped his zipper up against me every time he sang, whoa.

"Quit that," I said, but I didn't mean it, and then every

time the song got to that part he did the same thing, until the end. "You walk by, and I fall to pieces," and on the last note he leaned over and smacked his lips right by my ear, so close that I got goose flesh on my arms, and couldn't hear out of that ear for a few seconds.

Berenice's came into view. The roof was flat and the corners of the building were rounded off, and the windows were set into the walls at an angle which tilted out so that the place looked like a white tugboat chugging hard against the wind, plowing through the cars nosed up under the windows like a fleet of souped-up rowboats. The exhaust fan from the grill poured out smoke which smelled of cooking hamburger meat and rancid oil. A song I had heard before which told the story of a truck driver who had been driving for six days and was going to get home, finally, blared out from bell-shaped speakers attached under the eaves of the roof, and I remembered that my daddy was probably there, had probably put a quarter into the jukebox and punched up his favorite song. I told Johnny to get us past the place as fast as he could. He stopped playing with me and sped up, the bicycle lurching as he churned up the pedals. The door to the place was open, and as we passed by I could hear men and strange bells and buzzers and sounds like a repeating rifle and clicks and low rolls like way-off thunder.

"What are they doing in that place?" I asked Johnny.

"Just getting drunk and playing pool and pinball," Johnny said as if he were talking about little kids and marbles.

I pictured Daddy in there, and I wondered for a breath or two if he wondered about me. Then for a breath, I thought of Mother back home in the kitchen making something sweet for me which I was headed away from as fast as I could on

Johnny's bicycle. And to my ears, all those sounds coming out of Berenice's were laughing at each other.

I peeked out from under Johnny's arm to see if I could see my daddy's car among all the others, but I didn't see it, and for the briefest time I imagined Daddy was nowhere, and it didn't bother me. We passed by, and the music and noise from Berenice's began to fade away behind us, and ahead came the sounds from the four-lane, like static on the radio at first, then more clearly separate sounds—the steady, low roar of car tires on cement like the sound of the ocean before you get to it, and the loud burr of tractor trailers headed north and headed south, and once in a while the blast of a horn as loud as a train whistle—and all the time the sounds getting closer to us and us getting closer to the place where we would have to somehow get out there with all the traffic. I held tightly to the handlebars and just tried to stay still and small to make it easier for Johnny. We rounded a curve and could see the highway and the traffic going thick and fast in both directions as though it had never started and never would stop, and Johnny and I and the bicycle were nothing compared to that ribbon of motion that had nothing to do with us or anything except that we were all going.

The road dipped, and we picked up more speed. We were going so fast I didn't want to look. I closed my eyes, then I heard a long blast from a horn, and I expected never to see anything again, but then I felt the ride get smoother, so I opened my eyes and saw that we were out there. Cars whipped by us scrambling the wind and stirring up dust and smells of exhaust fumes and oil and hot rubber. I was afraid we'd be killed, and I wanted to tell Johnny to stop the bicycle and let's get off and walk by the side of the highway, but when I looked back over my shoulder I could see that this was the part he had been waiting for. His eyes looked sharp and as cold as a frozen nail file, and the muscles in his jaws were pulsing as if that were where his heart was. So I held on and he kept going, and I just decided that what could happen wouldn't and that we'd make it. I think that got us there as much as anything—me holding on and believing.

The next thing we saw was the fair. Up ahead of us it spewed out above the trees that circled the fairgrounds. We could see the top half of the Ferris wheel, its swings being thrown up out of the treetops, cresting over and then plunging back into the leafy froth, the dive-bomber flopping over and over like a pair of dolphins breaching in a rolling green sea. Faded flags and pennants flapped against the darkening blue of the late summer dusk. Other rides boiled just beneath the tree line showing only a flash of metal or a bit of color, and now and then a neon claw would raise up a squirming shape and send it shrieking toward the ground. As we got closer, we could hear the growl and retch of the engines that turned and twisted and flung the rides, and we heard amplified voices of a hundred devils, voices which we knew and recognized to be calling to us, urging us to come and pay and be delighted and amazed and sickened but not disappointed and at the least to see what we had never seen before, and all the time the fair churned like a universe, each sound telling and each glimpse showing a small part of everything that could be had and promising that there was nothing that could not be had whether beautiful or so ugly that we would wish we had not seen it, had not come, did not know. That was what I had wanted in the first place and why I had stolen from my mother and come with Johnny and let him pet me and do things to me that he shouldn't do and that I shouldn't have let him do. I just wanted what I hoped was in the world, and there it was, I bet myself, there beneath the August-hardened green of those treetops.

We reached the gates to the fair before I had stopped wishing we would. Johnny hid the bicycle in some bushes at the edge of the field across the highway where a man was charging seventy-five cents per car to park.

I got the wadded-up ten-dollar bill out of my pocket and put it on the counter of the ticket booth, where it bloomed like a flower before a dirty hand darted out from the space under the window and took it. The hand gave me back a fan of nine one-dollar bills. Johnny wanted me to divide up the money before we went in, but I didn't do that for fear he would take off on his own if I did. We passed through the gate, where another man stamped a black ink star on the backs of our hands. Johnny stopped to button up his shirt and comb his hair. I folded the money and put it deep into my pocket, worried that Johnny would want to spend it all on something I wouldn't understand. I planned to dole it out, never letting it be forgotten that it was I who had stolen it.

We did everything I wanted to do. First we rode the Ferris wheel, and my stomach was never with me but just in the swing behind as we rolled over and over, happy that the ground was a place you could leave and then wanting to return to it when from the top we saw everything that was down there. We went into the Scary House. But that wasn't a bit frightening. The witch in there was broken, and when she came flying out of a secret door shaking her broom at us her head fell over to one side. She looked like a drooling idiot. The real scare came when the door that was supposed to open didn't so that the cars piled up behind us, and the whole ride was shut down for a good ten minutes, and we sat in the hot dark and thought maybe we would die in there.

Johnny kept grabbing my leg trying to scare me, but it made me hard instead.

We rode the Tilt-O-Whirl and the Scrambler and I had to look down the whole time to keep from throwing up all the cotton candy and caramel apples and hot dogs I'd eaten. We went into the exhibit hall, where everything was bigger than it is supposed to be: tomatoes the size of cantaloupes and cantaloupes the size of watermelons and a watermelon as big as an oil drum.

In the sideshow we saw a little boy with flippers instead of arms and this person who said he was half man and half woman and didn't look like half of either one. You had to pay more and go to a separate tent to see it take off its clothes. Johnny wanted to go, but I held on to the money. We even talked to the alligator lady, who as far as I could see just had a bad case of dry skin, but she said she had played golf with Eisenhower and had had supper with Queen Elizabeth. We saw a fat lady dance the twist and a skinny man full of holes who drank water and then became the human fountain—a trick, Johnny said, but one we couldn't figure out—and we watched a colored man from Borneo eat a live chicken, which was absolutely not a trick, but was real and made me throw up all the fair food I had so far been able to keep down. Johnny and I had a long talk afterwards as we strolled along the midway trying to decide whether we would rather have been the chicken or the man from Borneo, and when we couldn't decide we got silly and started acting like we had acted on the bicycle. I saw people rolling their eyes and curling their lips and pointing at us. These two city boys asked Johnny if I was his girlfriend. He told them to eat s-h-i-t. We walked away, but Johnny got quiet again, and as we shuffled along with the fair crowd, I searched through the scrubbed-up farmers and jelly-haired rednecks and packs of proud city boys and bevies of khaki-shorted country club girls to find those whose arms joined them at the hip or neck or whose clasped hands linked them one to the other so that they blocked our way and we had to slow up behind them or squeeze past. I counted them in the crowd the way I would count bright dimes in a pile of dull pennies, and I came up with no more than a dollar's worth. I walked along the midway, counting those who loved as they should, and only able to love what I did and not what I ought.

While I was looking for those bright ones, Johnny slipped off or maybe just got lost in the crowd, and then I was by myself. I walked around the midway twice looking for him, and, not finding him, could find no place to be. I stood in front of a sideshow for a bit. I won a fuzzy snake by putting a quarter on a red 7, but I left my prize on the counter because I was the only one happy about it.

It got dark so I wandered down and stood in front of the hootchy-cootchy, hoping that I might find Johnny there. The girls were on a platform outside the tent. There were four of them in sequined dresses of varied and sickening colors—poisonous chartreuse green, nasty pink, school-bus orange and a purple color that reminded me of some candy Easter eggs I had gotten sick on one time. The sequins were bright on some parts of the dresses, around the zipper on one girl, on the skirt below the knee of another, but you could tell what the girls worked hardest. On those parts there were sequins hanging by a thread or rubbed off altogether so that their fannies and chests and bellies were just dull swellings.

A man with a microphone stood on one side of the platform and talked about what would go on once the girls were inside the tent. He tried to make it sound high-class and artistic, but the girls made sure that what he was saying didn't chase anybody away. They made rude faces, and they licked out their tongues as though they were being examined for tonsillitis. The men pushed forward right to the edge of the platform, and their upturned faces glowed in the light which spilled from the stage. One of the girls squatted down at the edge of the stage, and I thought at first she was going to the bathroom right there in front of everybody. I couldn't believe it, it was so rude, but the men went crazy and started hitting each other, and some of them started to climb up on the stage and almost knocked the girl over, so the announcer pulled back the curtain and the girls hurried inside, but not before each one had looked back at those wild men and shook some private part before she disappeared into the tent. The announcer went to the steps that led up to the platform, pulled out a roll of tickets from his coat pocket and began taking money from the men on the ground who, one by one, paid, then climbed up the steps and passed through the curtain. Soon I was standing alone, and the stage was empty and dark, and as raucous as they had been outside the tent, something inside had quieted them, for all I could hear was the muffled sound of a drum coming through the canvas tent.

 I left and got in line to ride the Ferris wheel again, but I had to keep stepping aside when my turn came because they wouldn't let me ride alone. An old lady brought a little boy up to ride, so they put me in the swing with him. I hadn't thought a ride on the Ferris wheel could last too long, but this one did. The little boy was scared the whole time, and he squealed so loud that it made me wish one of us would fall out. When the ride stopped he was still screaming and had his eyes clamped shut so tight he didn't know the ride was over. The carnival man had to pry the little boy's hands from the bar to get him out of the thing.

I walked around the fair for a while trying to find things that I could do alone, but there wasn't much. I was about to break down and call Mother, and let her take me home and do to me whatever she thought I deserved, when I saw, stuck out of the way over by the pony rides and the Pick-Up-A-Duck booth and all the other kiddie stuff, a tent that would have been red and white striped if it had been new. The banner over the entrance read, "See Tarzan, Master of Beasts." I walked up to the entrance to get a ticket from a man sitting behind a high counter who was trying to look like a woman, as far as I could tell. His hair was dyed yellow and poofed up like a piece of popcorn. He had on rouge and green eye makeup and his fingernails were long and painted black. There was a ring on every finger, big, rough nuggets of gold and smooth turquoise stones set in silver.

"Just one?" he asked, and his voice sounded like a woman's whose throat had been cut.

"Just one, please," I said, and he took the money, made a tear halfway through a red ticket and handed it to me. The face of a lion was painted around the entrance to the tent. I walked through the lion's mouth to see the show.

Inside the tent a scratchy recording of animal sounds played faintly—mostly birdcalls and now and then the roar of a big cat. There was a small circus ring in the center of the tent, and a spotlight shone down on nothing but the sawdust floor. I sat down right at ringside and waited for the show to start. There weren't many people in the bleachers, and I was thinking that they probably wouldn't have a show if some more people didn't come, when the ticket seller came in, looked around for a second, then walked across the sawdust to the back of the tent, lifted a flap and hollered, "Go ahead on and start." Then he walked back across the ring and out of the tent.

Tarzan ran out of the dark into the spotlight. He was dressed just like the real Tarzan, except that in addition to the usual leopard skin loincloth, he wore a belt with a pistol in it across his otherwise naked chest. He didn't look much older than Johnny, but really passed for Tarzan, I thought, good enough to be on television. He fired the pistol into the air, and a horse trotted out. Tarzan ran along beside the horse then leapt onto his back and rode around the ring twice, then he jumped off and took a bow as the horse trotted into the dark opening at the back of the tent. It didn't get any better for a while. There was a one-eared tiger that moved like an old dog. He did not so much jump through the hoop which Tarzan held up for him as step through it, and when his turn in the spotlight was over, he had a hard time getting up onto his pedestal just outside the light. Once he made it he curled up and went to sleep. After the tiger, there were some dogs dressed as clowns and then a flock of doves which were released from a net high in the top of the tent. After the net opened and the birds had flown out through the back, I counted three dead birds lying in the sawdust.

I would have left after that, but I felt bad for Tarzan. The crowd was so small. Nobody clapped or laughed, and a lot of the children were sprawled across their mothers' laps sleeping.

So I started trying to help him out. I laughed when something was supposed to be funny, and clapped for the feeble animals. Tarzan started coming over to where I was sitting whenever he got the chance, and he would smile at me then turn around and stand directly in front of me so that all I could see were his wide shoulders and barely covered backside. He'd wink at me when our eyes would meet, and one time I heard him say, "Watch this, sweet stuff," as he was about to make a little pink poodle push a baby carriage around the ring. I thought he was calling my attention to the dogs, but that wasn't it. It wasn't what I noticed. He made his backside jump in time to the music that was playing for the dog. I stopped watching the animals and just kept looking at him.

Until the elephant. It was the last act, and it was good. The dogs scampered out of the ring. The tiger got up and limped out. Then the music on the record changed to something just like an elephant would walk to, and out he came. He charged right to the middle of the ring and dipped his head, and Tarzan began shouting commands in what was meant to sound like a jungle language. The elephant stood on one leg at a time, first switching slowly from one leg to the other, then quickly in a rolling motion like a giant spinning top wobbling to a standstill. Tarzan touched the elephant on its trunk and it fell forward into a headstand, and kicked its hind legs in time with the music. Then it stood, shook its head as though being upside down had addled it, trumpeted and, flinging itself onto its back legs, stood straight up and marched in place. It finished off with a rhumba that purely shook the air, then bowed to Tarzan, and Tarzan made it come over and bow to me.

"Come for a ride," said Tarzan, and at first I thought he couldn't mean it, but he took my hand and pulled me out of my seat, and I stepped over into the ring. "Hold here," he said, and I slid my hand underneath the red leather harness that bound in the animal's knobby head. The trunk unfurled from beneath the elephant like something at the bottom of the sea, and the end of it encircled my foot. Tarzan spoke softly into the elephant's great, fanning ear, and the ground fell away under me. I rode through the air on a gray cloud above the quaking earth. We went once around the ring then floated out of the tent.

OUTSIDE IT WAS NIGHT, and in the shadows cast by the light of the midway, I watched as Tarzan chained the elephant's foot to a post. I looked back over the tent. Tracer lights on the Ferris wheel fluttered nervously, like birch leaves in the wind.

Tarzan lived in a little aluminum trailer behind the tent. It was hitched in front to a Cadillac the color of Pepto-Bismol and tethered at the back to a light pole by a thick black electrical cable.

"You really live in that?" I asked.

"In and around it," he said. He was running water from a hose into a foot tub for the elephant. All the time the animal was swaying as though to music only it could hear and searching Tarzan's body with its trunk, fondling his legs, moving over his chest and rustling his hair. Tarzan would laugh and pull the trunk away, but the elephant persisted like something blind in love.

"You're an old whore," Tarzan said as he slapped the elephant on the forehead. The trunk slid in between Tarzan's legs and underneath the leopard skin. He looked at me and licked out his tongue and grinned and winked.

"Can I see where you live?" Before I knew I was going to say that I had said it.

"How old are you?" Tarzan asked.

"Almost fourteen," I said.

HOME FOR THE DAY

I wasn't but twelve, but I couldn't say it.

"I don't know," he said. He looked at me as if he was looking for something in me, a sign or something, I did not know what, so I couldn't help him find it. I just stood there the way you do when there is no reason you should have what you've asked for.

"I want to see it," I said finally. I guess that was what he was looking for in me, those words or that willfulness. I climbed up the two steps to the door of the trailer and stood there for a second with my hand on the doorknob.

"I scored high on my achievement test, as high as somebody in the tenth grade," I said. Then I opened the door and went into Tarzan's house.

Inside the trailer was my ideal of real elegance. Everywhere was velvet, red and tufted, on the walls and covering the furniture. There were pink satin curtains on the little oval windows and fringed shades with a crystal teardrop on each pull. On the coffee table was a statue of a naked Roman and another statue of two naked Romans wrestling. One of the Romans had the other one right by his thing. Around the statues was a collection of glass elephants. I tried to pick one up, but it was stuck onto the table, as were the statues. Then I remembered what I had forgotten, being so dazzled by all the red and sparkle, that this was a house which had to move. I went over to the couch and sat down. It was so soft and slippery, like being naked in water. I heard him at the door. And then it was just me waiting for Tarzan, Master of Beasts, to come home from the jungle to our red velvet tree house.

He said, "Not what you thought it'd be, I bet."

"Better," I said. "It's better."

He said, "You look right at home."

"I won't tell," I said.

I promised not to tell, and I never have.

It was red and sparkly when it happened. I told him to take off everything, and then I would. He took off the loincloth, had to really, but he wouldn't remove the belt with the pistol.

"That ought to be the only way you'd do this," he said. I had not known that this kind of thing would have so many little details vital to it. At one point I had to change my promise not to tell to a threat that I would tell if he didn't keep going. So much of it didn't really feel good, and there was a lot that I did not understand. But it was all red and sparkly. There were long minutes when I didn't have to do anything but be still and look up into his face, and there were other minutes when I had to try and act like someone I thought he had in his mind. He liked it best when I acted as if I had done everything a hundred times before. What I liked best was all of it. What I didn't like was when it was over. He held me down, would not let me move, and I wanted to move. Then he made a noise that was like the noise I had once heard a horse that had been stuck in the mud for a long time make just before it died. Then Tarzan died there on top of me. I was sure that he had died, and I started to struggle to get out from under him, but he came back alive and held me still.

"No, don't move anymore," he said. "That's all she wrote." He rolled off me and fell back, as red and velvety as the couch we were lying on. I could not understand why he got up and put on that black shiny robe with the dragon on the back. Could not understand why he told me to get dressed or why he got so busy trying to get me to leave. I had never stopped wanting a thing just because I had gotten it. He had, but I did not know then what it was in that look of happy pain I had seen just before on his face, what was really to be heard in the awful, dying, horse-stuck-in-the-mud sound. I saw the moment, the perfect, red sparkly moment when at the same time as you get what you want, you stop wanting it.

I left him on the couch.

Outside, the midway was dark. The moon was full and at the top of the sky. The tent tops of all the amusements and shows stood out against the night sky like a city of churches. I heard the clinking of the chain around the elephant's leg, and I went to have another look at the big, beautiful gray thing that had brought me to Tarzan's red and sparkly place. I crept around to the back of the trailer and stood as still as the moon overhead, unable to believe that I believed what I was seeing. The elephant had broken loose from the chain, or had simply stepped out of it, but it had not run away. There alone and standing by the tent pole as though still tethered, with moonlight draped like a silvery blanket over its back and head, it was going through the exact movements of its act which I had seen before in the lion-mouthed tent. It was about halfway through to the big finish. All around was dark and quiet. It had been playing to no one. And now, in the moonlight, it played to me.

I NEVER TOLD Pete that story, but I told him stories like it. After we had been together for a while, sometimes it would take a story to get us going, to remind us that we could be a story ourselves. That went on for as long as it had to, until one night in the middle of gusto-filled sex induced by a tale of gusto-filled sex, he stopped what he was doing to me and propped up on his hands over me. Looking as though he had heard a knock at the door or someone call his name he said, "You're talking about us." I was. Somehow, after concocting tales from bits and pieces of longings and fetishes, of hopes and frustrated fantasies, I had finally come up with a combination that was actual. We had become our own inspiration, and from then on the trouble was over, and all it took was the telling of a fuck to enkindle another one. From then on, all I would have to do would be to mention a place or repeat a phrase—remind him of a piece of clothing, a time of day—and we would be twisted together. We had a name for it. We identified a behavior which we believed to be peculiar to us. We called it, of course, Pavlov's Fuck. It worked as if there was such a thing. Screwing became a self-perpetuating act, for when we did it, we did it fully and it was immediate, but also we watched in a way, as closely as if we had both floated up in the air and hovered over ourselves taking careful and detailed note of each move so that the one happening now could be saved and recalled. No, reconstructed. In the end, our lovemaking was an act of memory.

"That one was how it used to be" was what Pete would say afterwards. It was always as it had always been, until it had to stop. And when it stopped, as it had to, I didn't miss it so much knowing that it would have been as it was, if it could have been at all.

"I don't care so much," I said.

"I do. I mind," Pete said. He was sick when he said it. His hair, which had always been as blond and shiny as varnished pine, looked as if it needed dusting now. Two plastic tubes were coming out of his chest, and the ends, which were periodically hooked to the solutions that fueled what fight was left in him, dangled down on his stomach like loose reins to his heart.

After it had become a sure thing that I would have to, I told Pete that I didn't want to live in a world he wasn't in.

"I know," he said. "It's why I'm with you." At the time it made me happy.

In college I read that the life you imagine is your real life. I forget who wrote the book, but when I read it I took it for the truth. For the longest time, I imagined I could love imagined things, like God, but instead I fell for Pete. I dreamed up the kind of people I would have liked for parents. They left me in swank hotels attended by kind nannies while they lived for a time in Europe. That was as far as my imagination took me in concocting who they were. Most of the time I spent deciding who they were not. I was not the son of a truck driver or of a woman who could have done better but didn't. A woman who fell for sex, and since she was a good girl, never looked for it anywhere but where she found it the first time. She tells me these things.

"Why did you marry Daddy?" I hear myself asking.

Because he had a car.

We are sometimes each other's favorite toy, my mother and I. We play together, with each other or with one thing between us, or sometimes each other and something else. Today it is her hair. We are playing with it in front of her low, wide-as-a-Buick dresser. In front of this burled walnut monstrosity of downward curving surfaces, I comb her hair while she talks. We watch ourselves in the big round mirror that covers most of the wall in front of us, reflecting my mother and me and more of the room than we could see if we turned around and looked.

It was a green 'thirty-nine Chevrolet convertible. The first time I ever saw it was a Saturday in October, about nine-thirty in the morning.

From the plastic tortoise-shell box on the dresser she hands me hairpins.

I was raking leaves right out by the street, and first I hear this thing coming. I looked up from what I was doing to see it barreling right down the middle of the Avenue. Just a shiny chrome grin of a car. Your daddy had some trashy girl with him, and the two of them were sitting so close together that it looked like the car had a two-headed driver. Swerved over to the wrong side of the street and blew those leaves I had spent all morning raking right back into the yard. I had to drop the rake and hold on to my skirt to keep it from flying up around my head.

I am trying to do an imitation of Mrs. Kennedy's French twist, which I am having a lot of trouble with. Mother loves Mrs. Kennedy and looks more than a little like her. Mother's coloring is the same, from what we can tell by looking at black and white television and pictures in magazines, same dark hair and pale, clear skin. Mother is beautiful in the way Mrs. Kennedy is, and I think, and Mother agrees, that if they were side by side, and Mother was real dressed up and had her hair done by whoever does Mrs. Kennedy's, they could pass as cousins or something.

It should look like a very neat tornado, this French twist, but it's turned out the same size from top to bottom and looks more like a turd. Mother keeps turning her head to one side trying to see how the hairdo looks, but I can't let her see this mess.

"Then what did you do?" I ask. She'll talk and talk when we are playing with her hair if I ask her the right things, and don't make her look ugly. She thinks she is talking about herself, but it's Daddy I hear about.

Went right into the house and told Papa what had happened, and he got up from his chair and walked uptown to get what passed for the police here then. It was no use to it, of course. Your daddy was halfway 'round the world before Papa had roused himself up out of his chair. Later that same morning your daddy was back uptown, and went into Papa's store to buy himself a Pepsi. By then word had spread. What had happened to me was widely known. Just goes to show you how little went on here. Somebody hanging around the store knew who your daddy was and pointed him out to Papa. Papa went outside and found your daddy sitting on a bench in front of the store drinking his Pepsi. Papa told him he had two choices. Either he could come around to our house and apologize to me and see what he could do to make it up, or he, Papa, would have the police write him out a ticket for reckless driving, disturbing the peace and whatever else that might pop into his mind while he had his mind on it.

"Biggest mistake I ever made in my life, having him come apologize to you," Papa always said whenever he told about it. I have been working on the front. It has to be straight back off the face, but not slick. It's got to have height. I tease and rat. I smooth and back-brush. When I look into the mirror, I see her looking out. She has a studying look on her face, and I can't tell if it is me or the hairdo she is sizing up. I crouch, and bob, and now all my fingers are working in the French twist, trying to improve its shape. My elbows stick out. I think I really look like somebody who knows how to fix hair, and to fool her I put a look on my face that is meant to make her think I am working hard on something that will turn out to be wonderful.

"Give me one of those long hairpins," I say, urgently. She smiles and quickly fumbles in the box for the hairpin. She hands it over her shoulder. I take it and sneak a glance at her in the mirror to see if I have her fooled. She looks excited. She believes the hairdo will be beautiful, so I get her to talking again. "Then what?" I ask.

Oh! Well, here's what happened. It was just before lunchtime. Clyde Anderson had stepped across the street to see me and we were sitting on the porch in the swing. Mama had been hoping since I was born that I would marry Clyde. Clyde was all right. I was a junior and he was a senior and the only one in the whole school that I wasn't smarter than. Clyde was planning to go to the University of Pennsylvania and become a doctor like his father.

"And, that's what he did," I say, and she keeps right on talking as though I had not spoken.

So there I was with Clyde in the swing, probably discussing something Clyde thought was deep and I knew was stupid,

HOME FOR THE DAY

when I hear that car coming again. Thing fairly flew into the driveway on two wheels and squee-squawed around before it came to a stop like a dog settling into a dust hole. Your daddy got out before the dust had settled and floated up onto the porch in a cloud which he himself had raised. He was wearing this pair of butter-colored trousers that made you hungry for hand-churned ice cream, and a sky-blue shirt that had been starched and ironed to perfection. I thought to myself how he didn't look like the type who would make such a stir as he had. But then, he didn't sit down in a chair, he squatted there on the porch in front of me like he was getting ready to roll dice at my feet, which placed him, don't you see. Country boys of his type never sit in a chair if they can find room to squat instead.

"I know it!" I say. "Johnny will squat like that with ten empty chairs in a room."

I feel her scalp move, and then she twists slowly around to look at the real me and not my reflection. She is frowning. She is irritated with me. "What else," I ask. "What else was he like?"

Her face straightens out. Her eyes go gleamy.

Everything about him was long. Long fingers and long thin wrists, and these long legs draped in those buttery britches. So, he would do, you see, to say the very least, as far as appearances go. A picture of him would have been the best way to know him. It was him in person that made me dubious. And there I sat next to Clyde, a sure thing, and there was your daddy, a lot better-looking.

But what else, I'll tell you before you ask. Lacking in every way that I had been taught counted—a future embarrassment. So I focused on the car. It was shiny apple green with a convertible top the same color as those britches on your daddy, and I thought to myself how swell I'd look riding in it. I just sat there like a little rabbit trying to think how I would get from the porch swing to the front seat of that car.

Nobody said a word for what seemed like a solid minute, then Clyde leaned over and offered your daddy a handshake.

"Clyde Anderson," he said, like he was the King of England. Your daddy shot me a grin that would have been shy if he hadn't been so proud of his teeth. This lick of blond hair fell down on his forehead just as he was about to shake Clyde's hand, so instead he got busy fixing his hair. Pulled a ten-cent comb out of his back pocket and went to primping. I thought to myself, you think you're something to be as near nothing as you are.

"I know who you are," your daddy says to Clyde. "We farm a piece of your old man's land." Then I said something I ought not to have said, but it was Clyde's fault being there and telling me things that made me feel like I was better than myself and had a right to say snobby and rude things.

"Where did you get that car?" I asked, like I was the Queen of England. The way I asked it was so high and mighty, but I had to know because in those days dirt farmers didn't have cars like that one. If they came into town it was in a pickup truck that more than likely they'd had to run the chickens out of before they started it up, or in mule-drawn wagons, or they'd walk or stay home. So I felt like he was trying, don't you know. Clean and well-dressed with that car. It was Clyde who later said what I ought to have figured out myself.

"Well, Amy," except he didn't say well. He said h-e-double-l. "Any redneck who spends enough time in an outdoor toilet with a Sears and Roebuck catalogue can absorb at least the look of good breeding." Well, my feeling was that while every redneck might have a Sears and Roebuck catalogue in the outhouse, not every redneck had the sense to know how much better he would get along in life wearing those trousers and that blue shirt. Then Clyde went off on some tangent about how, in London, duchesses went around in old clothes, and how you couldn't tell a book by its cover, which I think you sure can. Such mess as that, and I simply said that Branch Creek, North Carolina, was not London, England, and if he couldn't tell the difference, then there was no use in our keeping company.

All your daddy said about where he got the car was that he had gotten it "from the gittin' place."

"Where's that?" I asked. He said if I'd come for a ride with him he'd show me.

"Did you go?" I ask, so caught up in her tale that I have forgotten they are married. Forgotten I am theirs. She laughs.

First, let me see my hairdo.

The time has come when, together, we examine what I have done. She picks up her hand mirror and holds it behind her head to see. Now we will decide, as we always do, whether, if she wore her hair in a way other than how she wears it, this would be one of the ways. Right away, she says she likes it.

It's just like Mrs. Kennedy's.

She is smiling at herself in the mirror and turning her head from side to side like a bird on a branch. The hairdo is not at all like Mrs. Kennedy's. That I haven't fixed that turd in the back is the least of it. It's just my messy imitation, my sissy boy pretending, and I can't help feeling disappointed in Mother for not being able to see how awful she looks.

After she has looked at herself for a while she reaches for a magazine on the dresser, opens it, and flips the pages quickly. She stops on a page with a picture of Mrs. Kennedy and the President all dressed up for a party.

Want to do another one?

This is what I love to hear, even when I have failed. I like the way her hair feels, and sometimes I can look in the mirror and put my face under that hair.

"Yes," I say. "I'd love to."

Here it is. This one. She looks like a princess. Mother places her finger on Mrs. Kennedy's face. All that shows is the hair. It is not the famous *bouffant*. In the picture, the hair is styled to look like the pillbox hat Mrs. Kennedy likes, but this hair hat is high on the top of her head rather than at the back, as is her usual style. There are soft curls sort of coming out of the hat of hair.

I start to take apart the sorry French twist. Hairpins rain down onto the floor, as I begin to brush out her hair. She takes up with her story, right where she left off, as easily as if she were reading it from a book.

Well. So, Clyde paled, and your daddy didn't get any worse than he already was, so I just made up my silly mind that if nothing else I would have a ride in that car. Then, just as I was about to say, "Let's go," out Mama comes quick-stepping through the screen door so fast the hem of her dress actually popped like a flag in a hurricane. Clyde stood up, of course, and Mama went to mincing and prissing to such an extent that it would make you pure sick. Your daddy didn't budge, and I thought, good for you. It didn't go over with Mama, though I have to blame her some for not behaving like maybe he might have some manners.

HOME FOR THE DAY

"I don't believe I know you," says Mama.

"I don't believe I know you, neither," says your daddy. I wanted to laugh out loud, but you better believe I didn't. Just sat there, waiting. I expected her at the very minimum to knock the tar out of your daddy.

But I don't know. Maybe it was because Clyde was there, and she didn't want him to see how she could be. All she did was smile like she was on the pot at a tea party, and your daddy was the guest of honor.

"Say that again," says Mama with that sweet smile about to break her face, it looked like.

Your daddy cut his eyes at me and grinned like that was just what he had wanted her to say. I was braced. Clyde just stared straight down at the porch floor. We had stopped that swing as still as if the chains had rusted solid. What was your daddy going to do, was uppermost on my mind. And what did he do? Jumps up out of the squat he had been in since he got there, straightens himself up like a dandy in a picture show and kisses her hand. I 'bout fell slap off the swing. Mama just stood there like Lot's wife for a minute. Then she jerks her hand away from his mouth, rears back and pops him across the face so hard that it echoed off the front of Dr. Anderson's house across the street. This of course messes up your daddy's hair, so he doesn't do a thing but pull that comb out of his back pocket and go to reprimping. When he's satisfied that he looks better than great, he puts that comb back in his pocket, nods politely as an undertaker to Mama and says, "Damned if I don't believe we know each other now."

Oh, it was good to me, though you would have never known by the way I just sat there like you do when you know you just have to let disaster fall into place. I mean, not even Papa *would have talked to Mama the way your daddy had. And as pure outrageous as it was, all I could worry about was that it probably meant no ride in that car for Miss Me.*

Well, Mama turns on me then. Wants to know if this is going to be a steady thing, what she calls a string of trash hanging around the house after me. Like I had stood out beside the street with my skirt up over my head hollering come and get it, rednecks. Made me mad as fire, and I decided then and there to do whatever I wanted to do about it. And you know, I had never done anything except just what I was supposed to do. But now it looked like I might be breaking bad, and Mama just became unbraced. It got pretty rank there for a while with Mama and me. She stopped just short of calling me a hussy and I stopped just short of deciding to be one. I looked to Clyde to help me smooth Mama out, but he took her remark about the string of trash to include himself and told her so, before he flounced off home. That about killed Mama more than anything I had done, for the Andersons were the only thing that even passed for highfalutin around here. But it was the convenient end of Clyde Anderson for me and good riddance, I thought to myself then, and, honey, I still do. Like to have sent Mama off in orbit though. So I figured the situation was about as cheap and sorry as it could be, and that if I was ever going to be any trouble to my family, might as well be now. I just got straight up from that swing and went into the house and tied a kerchief on my head. Mama right behind me blessing me out, until I turned on her like I was going to pop her and said, "Mama, I'm going to step up the street, and I'm not coming back until there is a quietus around here." She grabbed my arm and snatched that kerchief off my head. I didn't do a thing but go right on, bareheaded as a strumpet.

I have teased every hair on her head. She looks like she is under water holding a live wire. But she goes on talking, ignoring what has to be done to her before she can look beautiful.

"You march straight out there to the porch and send that boy back to the sticks before you go anywhere," Mama says, and I said fine like I didn't care one way or the other. Then I went back out onto the porch and told your daddy that in five minutes if I happened to be uptown and he did too, we'd see if I'd go for a ride with him. Lord, I ought to have been tied up and gagged. That was as good as your daddy wanted to hear, and it was the start of a whole lot of trouble which I took more than a little enjoyment from.

I met him uptown and went for a ride with him, and from then on the tongues continuously wagged. You would have thought I had stripped from the waist up and jumped up and down in the middle of Main Street from the way people carried on. Didn't bother me much, because I kept my own counsel and knew more or less what I was doing, which was just trying to stir my life up a little. And your daddy might not have been a gentleman as far as making a proper introduction of himself and carrying on a polite conversation, but he never tried any of the things I had been told a boy like that would try. Never even tried to try them.

You know where we went that first time? Drove five miles out into the country to where he lived.

"I want to show you to Mama" was what he said when I asked him where we were going. Wasn't what I expected nor wanted, but I can tell you that I have never before or since felt as welcomed as I did when I got out of that car of his and stood there in the yard of that sorry house where he lived, and passel of the ugliest, dirtiest, snottiest-nosed trash children, your own future aunts and uncles, gathered around me like I was a princess, angel, missionary. Honey, I knew I was pretty, but to that collection of poor little things I was a raving, merciful beauty. I was so wonderful I could even smell myself. With all of them unwashed and three or four of them in diapers that were so dirty they dragged the ground, all I could smell was the talcum powder I had put on that morning. Smelled myself, clean and blossomy in the middle of the worst squalor I had ever witnessed in my life. I have never been able to explain that, but it is the absolute weird truth. I mean, there was a hog parlor near about at the back door of the place, fresh chicken manure anywhere you wanted to put your foot down, and a mule lot across the road and, as I say, those stinking children. Miss Me, I stood there breathing in the scent of white lilac dusting powder. And I was not even in love with him yet.

He went into the house to get his mama, and those poor little young'uns went to pointing and poking at me. One clamped himself around my leg tight as a garter. I tried to give them all a pat or a little hug and then they were at me like flies to filth. What weren't hanging on were a few feet away cutting up a caper to attract my attention.

"I can roll over on my head," says this little blond one holding a biscuit, and off she went across the yard doing somersaults. That set them all to doing their tricks. The somersaulting one was the most complicated of the bunch. The rest hopped up and down on one leg or bent over and tried to stand on their heads, some of them hollering, "Look at me, watch this." The little ones who couldn't talk just squealed and jumped up and down.

It was just before getting out of hand when your daddy

comes back out of the house followed by this woman who looked like she certainly had given birth to every one of that pack and then some. Had another one wedged in between her hip and the crook of her arm. She looked like ten miles of hard country road. But then who wouldn't have, who had been through childbirth as many times as she had? Your daddy didn't look like he could have caused her to be in the shape she was. He looked like he had just appeared fully grown and groomed standing there amongst what he maintained was his family. You'd never know to look at them now that your aunts and uncles had come from such a monged-up mess as that, would you?

I didn't tell her that I thought I would know.

His mama stamped her bare foot on the hard dirt, and those children scattered. All except this little toddler who didn't have enough sense to. That was your Uncle Thomas. He stood there and peed like a little puppy dog.

"Go out yonder to the well and get this girl a cool drink of water," she said to your daddy. Then she put the one she was holding right down on the ground by my feet. She asked me to watch him. Said she was going into the house to get some "cheers for us to set on." The little scamp pulled this plastic banana off the toe of one of my shoes and went to trying to eat it.

Before long we were sitting on some straight-backed kitchen chairs drinking well water out of some no-handled teacups and chatting away like we had all known each other for years. Your daddy held the little one who had tried to eat the banana off my shoe. Him holding that baby was what did it as much as anything. There is something about a good-looking man holding a baby that makes him hard to resist. The baby acted like *he thought the world of your daddy, playing with his hair and grabbing his ears. I couldn't think of a thing except how I wished I was that baby with his hands all over your daddy.*

I am hearing more than I want to, now. "I'm finished," I say.

What? This is nothing like the picture. You couldn't get my head in a bushel basket.

In the mirror, I see she is right. The hairdo is the one in the picture only somebody set off a string of firecrackers in it.

Give me that brush. I'll never get this mess untangled. Go outside and find some boys to play with.

I just stand there watching her in the mirror trying to pull the brush through her hair. She grits her teeth and winces with pain.

Go on!

"Well, I wish you had married Clyde Anderson," I say.

She stops still, the brush caught in her hair, and looks up into the mirror at me. The next thing I see is the brush in her hand moving in a wide arc out from her hair. I am watching us both in the mirror when it hits me in the face.

I KNEW WHAT SHE MEANT about wanting more than anything to touch Daddy. But that day in front of the mirror, and for a long time after, I was ashamed of her and of myself. I felt that way until I met Pete. I came home from New York to try to explain, only to her, about Pete and me. To tell her that I too had found someone unacceptable. She tried to understand.

But don't tell your daddy.

On that visit home, when I was grown and happy in love,

she finished her story. She told me she had come to think that Daddy had taken her to his house that day to show her what she would be getting, to somehow forewarn her and give her the opportunity to avoid it, him, the life she was to have.

Just wanted me to know the worst, right off, I guess.

But Daddy knew what he was doing. No doubt, she saw just what she wanted to see. She was only half what she thought she was. He was half what she was. They were married by the summer after the fall they had met.

Do you know the worst that could happen with you and this Pete?

I am the fool who answered yes to that question.

I think of Pete and me, when I think of them. But he was all of himself when I met him. He just added me. And I never got any better or became any more than half anything. I was just added on, then left over.

It is hard to think of him as gone or lost. Rather, it seems he is something to come. My memories are in the future, like a dream so real, so good it has to be true. The worst has happened, but what frames the picture my mind calls up when I think of Pete and me is a time when we weren't sure, a time when it went wrong. That time measures my memory.

Once it went so wrong that it ended. He had only been gone a month, and I could put my hands around my waist. My breath smelled like my insides had died. I tried everything to get him to stay. He left. He said it was because he wanted to be on his own. I told him that anybody who loved me was on his own. It made him laugh, but it didn't make him stay. What I think is that it was that boy he wanted to go to bed with. Pete thought he had to get rid of me to do it. He did have to get rid of me to do it. It was honorable, the way he left me to do this thing, for in those days, people seldom bothered to get rid of whomever they were with if they wanted somebody else. This was in 1979, the end of the height of the time when, at least in my life so far, anything went. Pete and I were out of all that, but we saw enough to know what was going on, and we heard plenty from people who lived it.

So when he came back home that night from where he had been for a month, and I asked if he had missed me and he said no, my first thought was that he had fallen in with the times.

There was just that one time. When he came back, it was for good, and I never brought it up to him. I was too relieved. But I dreamed about it. I still do. I dream he is alive and has been unfaithful, and I wake from that dream full of visions. Laughing, sneering, unfaithful sex is what I see. Sometimes in the dream, I have found out that he has been unfaithful, and other times I'm there. I walk into a room, and there he is, impaled, and he looks up at me and laughs. Sometimes he is twisted with another man or lots of other men, and I wake up and wish he were alive so I could kill him. I never dream that he is with me. I think my mind has forgotten how to construct that in a dream. I think I am glad it has. I wish I could have good dreams about him. Good dreams are not so real. But those I do not have. What I have is what was. What was, as far as I care about, was seventeen years of—I don't know. Seventeen years of plain old life. Plain old life like most everybody else in the world. That's the best you ever get, as far as I can see. That's all you lose.

Whenever I try to think about this I get all tangled up, and what Pete and I had and what we were seems unimportant and ordinary, and I guess that's what it was. All I can think in my muddled-up head is that because it was ordinary and so like all other couples that I have known of or heard about, it was exceptional. If we hadn't thought of ourselves as singular, we would have been. We were so arrogant, thinking we were perfect. Thinking that how we had done it was the way and the only way to do it. And people would ask us how we kept it alive, and we would answer. We had plenty of advice to give, but none of it meant a thing or could help anybody if they did not, like me at least, care that wherever their eyes looked, there was that other person, or if they had not come to accept that they were not on their own, that they could never want to be. In the end we didn't help anybody stay together any more than we helped them to part. We were just there for anybody who was interested to see, floating above the common notion that there are no truly happy couples. We were happy enough.

So a picture of Pete then, knowing that a picture can't be drawn.

I wish I had written down things as they happened back then. I never did, maintaining that only the unforgettable deserved to be committed to the page so writing it down seemed a contradiction and might even encourage a loss of memory. It's always better in the head. And anyway, I didn't think I would have to rely on my memory so soon. I thought my memories were in the future.

What can I remember?

He was blond and sure of it, although his hair was light brown. He had confidence in anything that had to do with himself. He had confidence in his confidence. He had it in me. He believed he was taller than he was, though he was plenty tall, six feet, two inches. I was always reminding him what his height really was, the true color of his hair, the exact date of his birth. It was a game with us, like dickering over a price for something neither of us really cared about.

"You're thirty-six," I'd say.
"I'm thirty-two."
"Thirty-four."
"Thirty-three."
I'd let it be that. "And six feet tall."
"Six-three."
"Right. Have you had your hair streaked?"
"It's the sun."

There came a time when I couldn't remember his real age, a time when he looked taller to me than even he thought he was, and right now, as I try to picture him in my mind, it is a head full of hair as yellow as corn silk I see.

What else? A word, a phrase, the sounding of which will bring him back?

The best white tap dancer in New York City. That's what some called him. It was the word *white* which caused a disappointed smile to cross over his face as he received the compliment. For him that word was the limitation.

"If I was black, we'd be fartin' through silk, honey," Pete would say to me.

"Being white was no handicap to Fred Astaire," I said.

"He was the best dancer in the world," Pete said. "No other adjectives needed."

I don't know if Pete was the best white tap dancer in New York, but he was great, and if we didn't fart through silk, we farted all over the world through cotton.

Audiences fell in love with him, and I along with them. Whenever I saw him dance, which was nearly every time he did, it was as though I was seeing him for the first time. Not just seeing him dance for the first time, but seeing him. I'd sit there in the audience with my heart breaking. For when he danced, he went to a place I could not follow. We were separated by his talent, for it was the thing about him which I could not claim or partake in or keep private between us. It was something which even he didn't own. It left no mark. I have pictures of him dancing, but they rob what is essential to it, movement. And words cannot retrieve the effort or the effect of something drawn in space on a phrase of music and the silences between tones. If he owned anything about his dancing, it was simply the right to disperse it. When he danced he was off to a place from where he could not be called back, and I just had to watch and wait, hopeful that he would return. Except for that, it was like now. He was, in a way, dead to me, and I watched a vision of him through an invisible wall, thick as plate glass.

My crush on him was renewed each time he took the stage, and after the performance, I'd go back and wait with the others, craning my neck to see him and foolishly trying to find words to tell him how wonderful he was. I'd be the last one to leave, and could never believe my luck at being the one who left with him. The relief of that, like waking from a dream of heaven, happy I had seen it, but glad to be back.

We would leave the theater together, but leave in silence as though walking toward each other from a great distance. After a while he would speak first, and what he would ask me is still a riddle to me.

"Do you still love me?" he'd ask quietly, almost as if he had done something to hurt or anger me, confessed to an infidelity or suspected me of one.

"I still love you," I'd say softly. That question and the answer I gave each time were directions back, the distance between us crossed on feet as light as our hearts—a journey home ended.

I gave up my third-from-the-left-in-the-back-row career on the stage, and took jobs when we needed me to, but they were the kind I could abandon, always ready to follow whenever he went on the road with a show or abroad for a concert. Audiences paid happily for what Pete would have given them. I have seen them stand and applaud for a whole minute, an eternity in the theater. In Japan, I saw young girls faint in his presence. In Moscow, he was carried out of the theater on the shoulders of stevedores. We dined with a president and a queen, not at their table, but very near it. We had a good life going, lived among people and in places it would have cost us millions to do otherwise, and my full-time employment was making each day seamless for him. That's all I did, and I am proud of it.

I could tell a tale of letting others go first, of generosity, good manners, but it would not be about me. It would be about Pete and about dancing, about artistry. If my words could move in space, converse with music and rhythm, they still would not capture this particular dance and its effect. I am remembering a dance he made himself. It was for a musical comedy. In the dance, Pete played a hoofer, and this number is meant to be the hoofer's big turn. The scene takes place outside the stage door in the alley behind the theater, where the members of the chorus are resting between numbers. Downstage right, three men are playing cards. Others lean against the wall of the theater, talking, smoking. In a window above the stage door, behind a drawn shade, are the silhouettes of three show girls taking off their costumes, down to their camisoles. It is a hot summer night. The men are in undershirts. A woman comes out of the stage door and wipes sweat from her neck. She walks down left fanning herself with the hem of her skirt. One of the men playing cards begins to sing the words of the song. Pete, as the hoofer, has come out of the stage door and stands upstage center, in shadows, a towel draped around his neck.

I am in the audience. I am irritated with Pete because he is supposed to be singing the song, but he has given it away to this chorus boy. It is a typical musical comedy moment where the song has nothing to do with what eventually takes place on the stage. The gist of the song is that it is too hot to move. But of course, the dance is the thing.

They begin slowly at first, dancing steps which Pete has given them. He ambles around the stage, pauses at each group of dancers, demonstrates a step which they in turn pick up and begin to elaborate, detail, make intricate. It is some of Pete's best stuff, and he has given it to people who aren't good enough for it. Before long the whole stage is dancing and Pete moves from group to group, his hands in the pockets of his loose-fitting trousers, lightly directing them. He is the spirit of dancing here. I can see what he is up to now, but will he dance? He is deliberately making himself unimportant. I want to see him shine, gobble up the stage, take the light. But he does not do this. He joins in with a group, casually picks up their footwork for a phrase, then moves off to join another line, but at the end, unobtrusive, tacked on. Soon the stage is alive with bright light and twenty dancers, Pete among them, but not in a special light, just one of the gang. They are full front and tapping intricate patterns and rhythms which have the audience interrupting with repeated applause and calls. Pete has given each dancer a moment alone, a specialty. The audience is going crazy applauding each dancer who outdoes the one before him. The chorus ends in full light to a twenty-two-second hand so loud it's like standing at the base of a waterfall. When it dies down only Pete is left on stage. Now, I think, he will really show them something. I am waiting for him to clean up, top what has come before, as I know he can do.

The stage light is now low, affecting that of an alley at night lit by the glow of a city. Pete strolls downstage in a dim spot, holding the ends of the towel around his neck. He looks around the stage where the dance has been, closes his eyes and smiles to himself. Then he begins an easy soft shoe, one anybody could do with very little practice. The dance begins to turn and moves in a circle around the whole stage. He ends leaning against the stage-left proscenium arch. He throws his head back and laughs, then with his right foot performs a four-beat side riffle. To perform it the foot must move isolated apart from the leg with the speed of a hummingbird's wing. But to appreciate it, you have to know about it.

"You can list on fewer than the fingers of one hand the dancers who can do this," Pete had said to me the first time he showed it to me.

The metallic flurry still hangs in the air as Pete flicks the towel at the stage floor and exits. There is polite applause as with all such playoffs. The audience does not know what they have just seen or that it was Pete who had them in a frenzy of appreciation just moments before.

We walk back to the hotel together after the show.

"Do you still love me?" Pete asks.

"I still love you," I answer.

PETE DIED at home in my arms. The doctors tried to talk us out of it, but we were determined.

HOME FOR THE DAY

"Do you know what you're in for?" the doctor asked me after Pete and I had worn him down.

"No, and don't tell me" was my reply.

The day he came home from the hospital we tried to make it the same as when he came home from the road. I held him up, and we walked around the apartment looking at our things, just as Pete used to do whenever he came home after being away for a long time. He would pick up one of the wooden boxes he collected and fondle it as if it was a long-loved, lost pet found. He'd run his hand over a piece of furniture. We'd remember when we bought it and where. We appreciated what we had. Then we'd stand in the middle of the floor with our arms around each other surrounded by our things which we loved, not because they were especially fine, but because that was just how we saw ourselves, holding each other among our things.

"What a lovely home," I would say to him in a garden club lady's voice.

"Why, thank you. We like it," he would reply, politely.

We did that again on the first day back from the hospital.

The second day he began to vomit. By midday he could not make it to the bathroom, even with me holding him up. But he wasn't heavy. I carried him face-down, one arm around his waist and a hand on his forehead for support, like an urn. I stood holding him like that over the toilet until he was empty. It was like pouring dirty water from a large ewer. He thanked me every time, and once when I was carrying him back to the bed, he said, "I haven't been picked up by someone I love since I was a little boy. It feels good."

That night, he got better, and though his voice was not much more than a whisper, we argued over what most of our arguments had been about for the seventeen years we'd been together.

The morning of the last day, the skin on his back split, and I could see about an inch of his spine. All that morning, he called me Fred and spoke only tap-dancing steps.

"Fred," he'd whisper. "Step, shuf-fle-stamp, ball-change, ball-change. Hop shuffle step, fa-lap, ball-change."

I'd try to make up one, but he'd frown and weakly wave his hand, dismissively.

Before he died, he became lucid again. Basically he bled to death. Late in the afternoon, I saw a dark cloud, brown and red and black, spread out from under him on the sheet. At first, I tried to clean it up, but it kept coming so I thought I'd do it later. I just got in the bed with him, sat up against the headboard and pulled him up into my arms. Before long the sheets were soaked, and I could hear what was coming out of Pete dripping onto the floor.

Just before he went, he tried to crane his neck back to look at me, so I shifted around, still holding him, to where he could see me. His eyes twinkled mischievously, as though he had played a trick on me and was waiting for me to find out, and I thought I saw something like a smile on his cracked lips. Then they parted, and his tongue searched for the place where words were kept, and when it found a place near there, he spoke.

"Still love me now?" he asked. He sounded like a little boy who has done something bad but knows he is adorable anyway.

"Oh, yeah. Oh, yeah," I said.

It's women's work I do. On hot summer days when all the other boys are swimming or playing baseball or going howling-wild in the woods and fields which are running distance from anywhere in town, I slip away behind my grandmother's washhouse and arrange funerals. I spend long hours making caskets out of cigar boxes—humming somber but hopeful hymns. Since the time I discovered I wasn't a girl, but gave up anyway trying to join the race of boys, I have buried things. Dignified burials I give to frogs car-smashed in the street at night. Beetles, killed by DDT which is sprayed all over town by the county health department to keep down mosquitoes, rest in ground which only my imagination has hallowed.

In the waveless quiet of this real graveyard, I wonder what was the peace and happiness I found in my pretend cemetery. I wonder where it is. With its miniature mounds all covered with flowers picked from my grandmother's cutting garden and its tiny rock borders and tombstones easily chipped off pieces of slate which fall from the roof of my grandmother's house, this tiny cemetery is where I live on summer days, from the fleeting cool of the early morning until the cool returns at evening. And, I would say, happily.

Daddy does not know about my work, nor does my mother, but Grandmother and her maid, Lynn Dora, help and encourage me, saving boxes and cartons of appropriate sizes suitable for the burial of tiny corpses, and sometimes they supply the corpses as well. This morning, Lynn Dora came to me just after breakfast with a mouse, bug-eyed and creased at the neck, which she had caught in one of the traps she sets out the last thing every day before she goes home.

I can feel the damp rising from the moss-greened drainage ditch. I can hear Lynn Dora on the other side of the white-painted washhouse wall grating our dirty clothes against the washboard, and I hear water splashing, sloshing with a splat onto the stone floor, cascading from the pump into the metal sink, and then I hear the squishy and muted sound it makes after she adds the soap flakes. In the kitchen of my grandmother's house are sounds behind sounds. More water running to wash vegetables and the bright tinkle, like icicles falling, of silver forks and knives being taken from and put back in drawers.

Farther off, away in the wild woods and free fields, I hear the race of boys to which I do not belong, happy and sure, concerned with neither grief nor being so alive.

I am quiet, bent over a cigar box which I have decorated with paints which my daddy gave me to paint model cars, but which I have never used for that purpose. I line the casket with scraps of shiny, satiny cloth taken from my grandmother's sewing drawer, scraps which she has in such abundance that there are always others like them. Beside me on the ground is the poor dead mouse.

My miniature graveyard is a place of hardly any formality,

but it is a place where practical tasks are elevated to the level of ceremony—a place where care is taken and beauty happens. I have free run of my grandmother's cutting garden, and from the time when fresh tender sweet peas bloom until the time when asters and chrysanthemums, hard and showy, come to end the summer in bronze, mauve, yellow and maroon is the period which marks the season of easy sadness for me. Grief is only acted out, and there are no souls, so they are not lost. Just smashed frogs and dead rhinoceros beetles and sometimes a songbird or a baby sparrow which has fallen from its nest. Their passing is tragic only if I make it out to be. Here is a passionless solemnity and not that which will be required later in a world peeled and hollowed out. Here is a place where death is a memory of what has not yet happened.

Often, before they have been buried long enough to rot, I dig them up, brush the damp, clotted dirt from the top of the little coffin and look inside to see what it looks like to have been dead and buried. Then, satisfied with having seen into the grave, I reinter them with fresh ceremony and new flowers. Once, I dug up a frog which I had buried two weeks before after finding it frozen by a late spring snow. In the warm morning light, it blinked then stirred, then hopped out of the coffin, out of the grave, across the dewy grass. It was a miracle, I thought, and I knew then that what they told me in Sunday school was possible. Christ had risen from the dead not because he was the Son of God but because it was possible. My frog had done it.

Though Daddy doesn't know what I do here behind the washhouse all day long, when he returns from the road he brings me presents which, if I let them, would distract me from my little ceremonies. The enamel paints were a gift from him, meant to go with the model cars and trucks which he brings. The paints have been useful, but the model cars are of no interest to me except for the parts which are meant to be thrown away. The small pieces come attached to little plastic grids and once I break off the steering wheels, dashboards, tires and hubcaps, with what is left I make fencing for my cemetery which looks like the real thing. I have a box full of car parts, unassembled and all mixed up. They don't make model hearses. I have looked. I tried to make one up out of the parts I have. But I am not clever enough. The mistake I ended up with looked like what the Cadillac company would do if they made dump trucks. It just wasn't the thing which is called for.

Daddy gave me a toy gun and holster set which I have torn apart. The metal studs and pearly buttons make perfect little handles for my caskets. I keep this toy junkyard hidden away here at my grandmother's house underneath some tobacco canvas which she uses to protect her flowers from early frosts and which is stacked in the loft over her garage. I am always afraid that Daddy might ask to see a put-together car or offer to play cowboys with me but he has not. Still, I cover my graveyard of small animals with an orange crate, and put a heavy brick on it every night to keep him from finding it. Not that this is anything like a real way to hide it, but the disguise looks like something my grandmother would rig up to keep the dogs out of her rooting bed.

Lynn Dora comes out of the washhouse, carrying a pail filled with soapy water which she flings across the lawn. I am making a bed of gardenias in the bottom of the box for the mouse to lie on. She comes over to where I am and watches as I put the mouse down on the bed of flowers.

"You sure do put 'em away pretty," she says. "When my

time come I hope you there to put me away as pretty as you do your pests and varmints." She is obsessed with how she will be put away, as she calls it, or rather who will put her away, which she has led me to accept is the same thing really. She killed her husband, James, who got to drinking bad and beat her, and although she has two children, a boy and girl, who she put through college on what little my grandmother pays her, they will have nothing to do with her now. Her girl is a lawyer in Washington, D.C., and the boy teaches history in a college up there somewhere, but Lynn Dora says just because she won't sit in the front seat of the car with a white person and because she thinks Mr. Martin Luther King ought to hush, her children are ashamed of her and mad at her. They haven't been to see her since they got their education out of her. "I don't want them coming back whem I'm dead, pretending like they're sorry just because it will look good" is what she always says about them. So it will fall to some of us to bury her when the time comes. She wants me to do it. She has come to this decision based on what she sees of how I have made my little graveyard. And on the likelihood that I will be around when she dies. She doesn't want my mother or grandmother to have anything to do with it.

"Left to either one of them, I'll be slap in a cheap velveteen casket, the lid slam shut, and I'll be put away like you would somebody who'd killed hisself. I won't rest that way. I know I won't. A funeral supposed to make up for life. Ought to be pretty and if you wasn't somebody, let the world know that you had wanted to be. After I killed him, I put James away fine. Put him away just like if he had been there to do it hisself."

I saw how she put him away, as I saw how she killed him.

It was the day of my grandfather's funeral, and I had been taken to Lynn Dora's house. She was in an ill humor that day —fussing with James because she didn't want to look after me, but wanted to attend the funeral. An invitation to a white funeral was considered by Lynn Dora and her friends to be a prestigious one. So it was too bad for James that he picked that day to get drunk and go to beating on her again. I thought it best to go as unnoticed as possible since she probably would have been invited to the funeral if they hadn't needed her to take care of me. So I had gone way back in the field at the edge of the woods behind her house looking for maypop fruit. That's where I was when it happened. I could see her house, in the distance no bigger than a doghouse, and from time to time I'd hear the two of them yelling. Occasionally, too, I'd hear what could have been a pot hitting the wall, and several times I heard what I thought was wood splintering. Once I definitely heard Lynn Dora holler something that sounded like help me, Jesus, but I didn't pay much attention to any of it. Grandmother always said that half of what Lynn Dora and James said and did to each other was a lot of carrying on anyway, and had been pretty much a steady thing ever since she had known anything about either one of them. I had been taught to ignore it. But when I heard glass breaking I turned quickly and saw one of the front windows explode out onto the front porch.

James came flying out the window, rolled off the front porch into the yard and scrambled to his feet. He had just stood up when Lynn Dora appeared in the doorway. She was carrying the hatchet James used to split kindling wood. She was round and hard as a bowling ball, but regal in an unhurried way, and she carried the hatchet not raised but held lightly in both her hands as though she was carrying some tribal staff of office.

James took off around the house, running for what turned out to be his life. She pursued, as they later called it in court, but was too heavy to make a race of it, let alone catch him, and I watched as he ran faster and faster around the house, gaining ground until he came up right behind her. He was about to lap her, but he was looking back to see if she was on his tail and ran into her. She whirled around and raised the hatchet over her head and swung down, but he saw her just in time and jumped back, and that time the hatchet sliced air. He turned around and really raised the dust. She followed, and got around the side of the house, then she was stopped still and stiff with what she has since confessed to me was the best idea she's ever had. She cocked her head, and I feel as though I saw the plan come into her brain. She turned around and started running the other way around the house. They were going to meet head on, and James was about to fall for the kind of trick you see in a cartoon. The fool didn't have enough sense to just strike out across the field where she could never have caught him. When they met again he tried to turn around and outrun her, but she was ready. The hatchet was raised, and as he whirled, she caught him right in the back of the head. That ended the chase. She let go of the handle and the hatchet just stayed there stuck in his skull. Then he slowly turned to face her and the hatchet fell out of his head and landed down at his heels. He had sufficient life left in him to have the strength to yell loud enough so I could hear, "Damn, Dora, you killed me with my own hatchet," and to slap her across the face before he fell over backward. She kicked him as he lay on the ground dying. Then she got down beside him and shook him. When he did not come to or even stir she hauled herself up and looked all around the yard, then across the field where she saw me. She called my name, and I hollered back, "What in the world have y'all done now?"

"Run tell your grandma I killed James," she yelled.

The whole thing had seemed like one of those cartoons they showed before the picture show started. It must have been that it was so far away. I thought to myself, yes, ma'am, Miss Lynn Dora, I'll go tell Grandmother that you have killed James, but I am sure not going to sprint all the way up this dusty path into town in the hot sun. I'll run till I'm out of your sight, then I'll walk if I feel like it.

I started out at a good trot, but when I got out of sight of Lynn Dora I stopped running and strolled along comfortably and started to think just how I would tell what had happened, and the more I pictured myself telling it, the more I wanted to get there to do it, the more the idea thrilled me. I started running again.

I turned up the Avenue. Cars were parked on both sides of the street, and I could hear somebody playing "Abide With Me" on Grandmother's piano. I had forgotten that they were having Grandfather's funeral.

A big black hearse sat at the edge of the street in front of the house. The yard was full of people, black and white separated by the walkway which led from the street to the front porch steps. They were standing quietly and gazing at the front of the house as though they were waiting to hear an important speech. None of it made me think, Funeral, or Grandfather's dead in there. None of it looked sad. It looked like an inauguration. The people seemed interested, as though some very special visitor, maybe an unmet relative from far away and very different from us, was soon coming out to address them.

I stopped for a moment and just looked at them all. I noticed everything about them, and in a way which I had never noticed before. I made myself look at them as though for the first time, for I had convinced myself on the way that this was to be my most famous moment, and I wanted to remember how to tell it for as long as I lived. They were not just the people of the town and my relatives anymore, or simply friends of the family. They were my audience gathered, dressed in their best waiting for me.

Those in the yard were mostly people who lived on Grandfather's lands. The men wore dark shiny trousers and white shirts buttoned up to the neck and only a few had on ties. The white women wore dresses which had not been chosen for their appropriateness to the occasion but because they were the best these women had, so that bright and flowery summer prints shone among thrift-store wools and cast-off and hand-me-down tweeds. But the colored women all wore black from head to toe. Where the white women were hatless, the colored standing all together were a black pool, hats bobbing like flowers floating on a wind-rippled water. Shiny lacquered straw or cocked felts, satin-banded and topped with iridescent feathers, perched on their heads. Crow's wings and black rooster tails fussed in the breeze. Tulle veils misted over the women's deep brown faces like little clouds of soot.

On the porch, folding chairs had been set up on either side of the front door, and two congregations made up of the people of quality and Grandfather's business connections sat facing each other as still and expressionless as though nothing was or would be happening. The windows were open so that all could hear and those sitting near could see some of the service.

I walked through the crowd in the yard, climbed the porch steps and stepped into the doorway. Inside the house, more folding chairs had been set up in both the parlors and along both walls of the hallway, leaving an aisle which led up to Grandfather's casket.

The preacher, framed behind in a square of light paneling where the *Horse Fair* print had hung since the last time he was at the house, hovered on the landing above the assembled friends and family. Below him at the bottom of the stairs lay Grandfather, tufts of white satin nestled around his body and frothing over the sides of his open casket like a boll of cotton exploded and ready to pick. Embalmed, Grandfather looked as he had in life—irritated, impatient and stiff.

None of it seemed in the least bit sad to me or even purposeful any more than my own funeralizing out behind the washhouse, and even when I saw Grandfather in his casket, his chin on his inflated, indignant chest, death remained a plaything.

I did wish I had washed and changed my clothes, though. I had what Lynn Dora called tater ridges of dirt in the creases of the skin on my neck, and my knees and elbows were rusty-looking. I had eaten a grape Popsicle that morning, and it had melted and dripped down the front of my T-shirt. My shorts were dirty and as wrinkled as an old paper sack. I looked like something my family had tried to hide that had gotten out.

I started up the aisle between the folding chairs toward the front row, where my grandmother was sitting. Heads turned as I passed each row, and I heard a lady say, "That's his little grandson, the little poor little thing." They noticed. They pitied me, I hoped. It was a feeling so like love that only when I found love was I ever satisfied again.

What I had to say, the news, bubbled and frothed inside me. I was ready.

The aisle leading to where my grandfather lay in his casket was straight and narrow. At its end was where I would tell it. Where I would see shocked women gasp for breath. Maybe some would scream. I would watch as steady, purposeful men rushed out to help what couldn't be helped now. For the time it took me to get up to the front row where my grandmother sat, her face pale and papery as a wasp's nest, shrouded underneath black, satin-edged silk, spreading strife was my greatest glee. My happiness was complete, poised between the knowledge of what I was about to tell and what my news would cause to happen. Wild eruptions of uncontrolled hysteria were what I wanted to see there in that red-velveted, dark-paneled, calling card of a house. Women yelping, men falling over each other to be the first on the scene. Mine would be the clear, mean, calm, tiny voice of chaos. The havoc I would bring and leave behind would be greater than myself.

I was right behind Grandmother, and I thought how in the next instant only Grandfather would be as he was now. I stood there a second longer thinking that when I spoke, which would be with the next breath I took, my words would be remembered and repeated by all present for as long as they lived. Each would tell, his voice tight with outrage or frothy with glee, the listener slack-jawed with wonder or lips stretched in laughter, how on the day of Mr. Huland Lamm's funeral, his grandson, barefoot and in grimy shorts and a grape-Popsicle-stained T-shirt, walked into the middle of the hall of Mr. Lamm's house in town where he was laid out to be eulogized, and where all the relatives and townspeople had foregathered, and announced that the beloved and faithful longtime employee of Mrs. Lamm, Lynn Dora, had split open the head of her husband, James, with his own hatchet, which he used to chop kindling wood, and killed him in the front yard of the tenant house owned by Mr. Lamm which the two of them had shared since before they were married.

Some would marvel at my innocence. Others would revile me and pity my helpless family.

That day would be the day of reference for all other events in their lives, and they would relate other stories as having occurred not long after that time or just before or years after.

The preacher was reciting a poem. "Sunset and evening star,/And one clear call for me!" I took a breath big enough to tell my news. "And may there be no moaning of the bar—"

"Lynn Dora killed James," I said, but my voice sounded no louder to me than if I had been talking to myself.

"When I put out to sea," the preacher went on. "But such a tide as moving seems asleep,/Too full for sound and foam—"

"Listen to me," I said, loud enough that Grandmother turned her black-veiled face to see who was talking.

"Twilight and evening bell," he went on, accustomed to years of ignoring anything but the sound of his own voice, which he had trained to a pitch and volume sufficient to drown out crying babies and cut through the shrieks of grief-crazed widows and the whistle and rumble of the ten-minute-long freight train which rolled through the middle of town every Sunday morning.

"Listen to me," I said again. "I've got something to tell you." But if they heard they did not listen, for Grandmother rose from the widow's seat in the front row, came and got me and led me to the empty chair beside her. She put her arm around me, and with her gloved hand pulled my face into her side. From underneath her veil, heavy tears fell on me. I felt them drop on my head and slide down the shafts of my hair, cooling my scalp, hot with shame.

"I told them they should have let you come," she said, the glove now smoothing my hair. "They shouldn't have left you out."

And my news was lost with that.

I couldn't find my voice that day at the funeral, and the thick, high, impenetrable wall which Grandmother's grief, real and ritual, had built remained standing. The timid, devilishly self-important voice of a boy ignored was what bounced off it back to me as I burrowed deeper into the black, rosy smell of Grandmother's mourning clothes. After a while, the voice of the preacher, whining on about Grandfather being in heaven, put me to sleep. I dreamed I was standing on the front porch of my grandfather's house. In the yard was the same crowd of townspeople who had gathered for his funeral, and I, gazing out over their heads, spoke the words of a poem of my own composition. The poem was a long one, perfect, eloquent and of deep significance. During the recitation, people shed tears and when I finished in a simple, quiet voice of high seriousness, there came from the audience gasps, and then cheers.

I slept through until the funeral was over, and when I awoke, I could remember not a word of the poem I had spoken in the dream. I have never recalled a word since.

They found out for themselves about the murder, and then they did not believe me when I told them all that I had tried to tell about it at the funeral.

We buried James the following Sunday. Lynn Dora, wearing Grandmother's veil, sat on the front pew of her church with a nurse on one side and the deputy sheriff on the other. We sat behind her. She grieved as hard as a young, happy wife would have, and at the graveside, she got loose from the deputy and jumped into the hole with James' casket. The deputy went in after her, cursing her and all colored people.

When I insisted that I had seen the murder and had tried to tell them at the funeral, Grandmother told me that if I had seen Lynn Dora kill James, I would have to tell it in court, and that she would surely be put in the gas chamber, and did I want that? I lied, and said all I had seen was a fight, but not the actual murder. That, I hope, helped her case. But it was Grandmother's haughty insistence that James had brought about his own murder that saved Lynn Dora from the gas chamber. Grandmother's word, and the fact that they didn't care if James was dead or if Lynn Dora had killed him, were enough for the judge and jury. The plea was self-defense, the verdict not guilty. It didn't even take them the whole morning.

We walked out of the courtroom in procession. Grandmother led the way looking disgusted, as though she had just cleaned up where a dog had messed. Lynn Dora, holding me by the hand, followed. At the courthouse doors, she leaned down to me and winked.

"And that's what *I* like about the South," she whispered.

"WILL YOU SIT here all day?"

I have not heard her coming. The voice I know. It is the woman I met here before, all that time ago before Pete died.

It is as if this is the afternoon of that morning then, and just a day has passed since she came to see if I was somebody who might take an interest in the place. She is standing in the same spot as before, but now the sun is full in her face, and her shadow stretches out behind her.

"We cleaned the place off, but as you can see, it has grown up again," I say.

"It is you!" she says.

"How did you know?" I ask. "How could you tell from such a distance?"

"Well, I couldn't, but I told Lester I was coming over here to see who it was had been sitting out there in the graveyard all day long. He told me to mind my own business, but that don't never stop me. Then halfway over here, I remembered that day you were here before."

"That was some time back," I say.

"Was it? Well, I remembered it on the way over here, and I just said to myself, I wonder if that *is* him," she says.

I smile and look away. For an uncomfortable time, we are silent. I look back, and smile again, hoping that she will take that and my silence as a wish to be alone.

"I had a sister who sat all day long, day after day in the graveyard where her husband was buried," she says, pushing up her glasses then folding her arms. She looks off toward the far woods as though to collect and arrange the events which she is about to relate, and I begin to worry that hers is going to be a long story. But when it comes the next sentence is short and the end of the tale. "She was down there beside him inside of a month," she states flatly.

She does not intend to give a story, maybe, but to take one?

"What is it down there?" she asks, nodding to the small bare patch of earth at my feet. "I know, or know of, most everybody in this county. There h'ain't been a soul buried here in the last twenty years that I didn't see put down. What you got buried down there, a little dog or something? Ain't a baby, is it?"

"No," I say.

"Didn't think so. You don't look like a daddy. Some people can be just as curious and particular about a dog or a cat as they would be over their own children. I like to never got over it when I lost my little Peanut. You can get attached to the onlyest things." She chuckles, and looks off toward the woods. She sighs. I do not speak.

"Had a cousin who went nuts when her washing machine broke down past fixing. Ended up flat on her back in a bed of grief over an old wringer-type Kenmore."

I cannot help paying attention, and I look up at her and smile to let some steam out of the laugh that is on the verge of bubbling over in me. She claps her hands together, "It's the truth," she says, and laughs and I giggle and shake my head, and for a moment we two are bound together by our good sense. We know what's crazy. We are sane, amused, astonished together for a moment.

"Did she let them throw it out, after it—you know—died?" I ask, and we can't stop laughing because we both think that word *died* is the funniest word we have ever heard. "Or was there a service of some kind?" I ask, and that kills her. She lets out a whoop that rattles a bevy of quails from the underbrush, and sets a dog off somewhere on the other side of the woods. Then in a heartbeat she shirrs her brow and sets her face in an attitude of mock gravity, and her eyes take on the twinkling assurance of a professional comic. "No, not right off," she says. "At first she let it stay right there on the back porch. Just unplugged the thing, left it like it was, full of clothes floating in soapy water. But it was high summer and too hot to even fan yourself, so in a day or two that water was smelling high and breeding mosquitoes. Still, she didn't show the first sign of sense about the whole business, and every time her husband tried to talk to her about having the machine—what would you call it?—laid to rest, we'll say, she'd have a fit of crying and retreat deeper into her grief. Wouldn't eat or get out of bed to wash herself or rake a comb through her hair or so little as kick a path through the dirty clothes that were flung all over the house. And it was the busiest time of the year, what with the tobacco crop ripe having to be got out of the field or lost. Her husband and children working hard as they could every day in the same nasty clothes, just adding filth to filth, until finally every one of them was going around all but naked save whatever they could find to wrap around their private parts. Of course, she didn't raise herself up to cook a mouthful for any of them to eat, so it was tins of anything that comes in a tin, and Pepsis, and screeching toward pellagra and rickets for the whole crowd. I did what I could, toting over what we had left up there to them, and when I'd poke my head through the door of her room to tell her what I had brought, she didn't say thank you or kiss my foot, and I felt like she even resented it sometimes. But I guess she had at least a remnant of concern for her children, for she never did tell me not to bring any more. But one day I went up there with two fifty-pound fertilizer sacks to gather up their clothes in so I could take them home and wash them myself. I wasn't going to tell her what I was up to, but slipped in through the back door and tried to go about my business as quiet as I could. I hadn't ever seen filth like that in my life and haven't since. The dirty clothes were just the bottom layer. They would have been living cleaner in a ditch. But I fell in and worked it like a maggot in corruption, and was making out fairly well. Then I was clawing my way through a pile and uncovered where their old mama cat had deposited a litter of kittens and gone off and left them. She had not been able to find them again, and every one was dead and starting to rot. I don't remember exactly what it, was I exclaimed, but it was loud and rousing, and the next thing I saw was her standing in the doorway looking like somebody escaped from the crazy house holding this bright orange, plastic baseball bat over her head to hit me with.

" 'Estelle, put every scrap of what you got in them bags back where it was,' she said. Well, between nearly choking on the sight and stench of the place and being faced with a nut-brain fully able and wanting to beat me to death with a baseball bat, even if it was just a toy, rather than let me touch another thing in what she had evidently decided was her memorial to that stupid broken-down wringer washing machine, I just lost the will to assist.

" 'Honey, enjoy your misery' was all I could think to say to her. I flung the contents of those two bags to the four foul winds in that room and then backed out of the house. When I got into the yard, her husband was coming in from the field wearing a pair of overalls covered with the evidence of one full month of life nowhere near soap and water. 'Ed Oscar,' I said. 'It's plain as day that that washing machine or your wife, one or the other, has to be carried away from this place.' I came right back to home and washed not only my hands but my entire house from ceiling to bottom porch step of the whole business. I did keep toting food up there in whatever containers I could find that could be left, but I'd just put it someplace high on the back porch and covered against the general filth which had extended to even the air surrounding the house, and then I'd flop right back home.

"Well, I found out later that Ed Oscar had leaned his mind in the direction of a remedy after I left that day. Said her thinking she could do damage to me with a plastic baseball bat had convinced him that something had to be done. Dirt and regular craziness, he said, was one thing, but her ready to possibly murder for the sake of that machine was headed off towards tragedy. What he said won't sense but it was near enough to it. Plus the washing machine had started to breed frogs, which none of us noticed until it was too late. Was me that discovered them. One day everything was the same. By that I mean the filth was at the same plateau it had reached after a month of her mourning. Next day when I went up there—this.

"Nobody but her went near the machine. She would shuffle up to it like a widow to a casket and just lean over it and peer down into the tub and add her tears to the slime. So me nor Ed Oscar, neither one knew that the thing had been squirming with tadpoles for some time. The place was a torment of little frogs not fully grown, but big enough to have crawled, hopped and scrambled out of the festering swamp inside the tub of that machine. The back porch was simmering with the vile things, and poor Ed Oscar was sweeping them out of the house and had this wild look in his eyes like anybody with any sense would have. And her, standing in the middle of the infestation, laughing. And not a laugh that saw anything funny in the situation, but this crazy cackle that just strummed your nerves. When she saw me, she clapped her hands and jumped up and down and the floor shook and set the frogs boiling around her feet. "It's come back to life!" she said, then ran back into her room and slammed the door so hard every one of those frogs jumped in unison. All Ed Oscar could do was cry and sweep and say, 'Oh Lord, oh Lord,' right steady.

"Well, I had to go get involved again. 'Ed Oscar,' I said, 'you go prop the strongest chair you got against the door of that bedroom, and then get back out here and go to sweeping.' I got the rake and pitched in to help him. We raked and back-raked and kicked them with our feet and made about as much progress as we would if we had been raking marbles uphill. Whichever way you sent them they would come back at you like waves washing up on a beach, and the sight of their motley little backs and white bellies tumbling around and peeing like to made me sick. Would have if I hadn't got so mad. Finally I got the hoe and stood on the ground and pulled them off the back porch and Ed Oscar got the shovel and scooped up load after load and threw them off the end of the porch into the grass. In a day or two there was no visible sign of them but come nightfall the croaking and peeping would near about run you crazy.

"We took to feeding her through her bedroom window, which Ed Oscar would nail shut with a new ten-penny nail every time we had to open it to poke her food through. She ate about every other meal, the rest we'd hear her pitch against the wall. But she never once complained about being locked up or asked us to let her out. Between feedings we would discuss what to do. I was all for calling the state hospital and handing her over to let them help her if they thought they could, but Ed Oscar said he just didn't feel right about doing that yet, not until he had tried getting rid of the machine first.

"One Saturday morning I got together a pair of clean overalls and a shirt of Lester's and carried them over for Ed Oscar to put on, and he set out for town and Cline Brothers' Appliance Store.

" 'Get the nicest one you can afford, Ed Oscar,' I said, 'and see if they'll give you something off on a trade-in of the old you-know-what'—I said that behind my hand. He climbed into his truck and drove off.

"I sat down on the front porch by her window and waited and watched the children play in the front yard. They'd got so ragged and smeared with dirt from all the neglect that they looked worse than terrible. Their little underpants were hanging from their waists by the elastic like something you'd see on an Indian. She went to roiling and bumping around in her room. Her addled mind was on to us and working was what I was afraid of, but I couldn't see a thing when I looked through the window it was so dark inside. I was scared to open it.

"Along about noon, Ed Oscar's truck turned off the main road racking up a cloud of dust behind it. Looked like he was trying to outrun a tornado. He trotted across the yard in a frolic and jumped up on the porch.

" 'I got one that looks like something from Mars and does everything but put your clothes back on for you,' he said, so excited he forgot to whisper. 'And they give me ten dollars off for the trade-in of the old one.'

"She heard him say that and raised a commotion that sounded like a cat shut up in a shoe box. I just rolled my eyes.

"What would she do when they came to take away the machine and bring the new one was uppermost on our minds. Next most was how in the wide world we were going to clean up the old machine without her probably trying to kill us. Ed Oscar had told the salesman at Cline Brothers' that it was in good condition, just old, but still had a lot of use left in it.

"They were coming on Monday to bring the new one and cart off you-know-what. I knew in my mind that whether or not we would do what we would have to do to her to even get near the thing was something only Ed Oscar could decide. I laid it right out.

" 'Ed Oscar,' I said, 'you know as well as I do that we are going to have to tie her down tight.' All he could say was 'Oh Lord, oh Lord.' But I had made up my mind and was letting it work. 'Go out there to the barn and find something good and strong,' I said.

"He started off toward the barn with his chin near 'bout down on his stomach. 'How did it get so far?' he asked the ground.

" 'That's something only you and her and the Lord in Heaven knows, Ed Oscar,' I says, though I had my theories, which were a mixture of possibilities having to do with how poor they were, and her lifelong tendency towards stupidity, set aboil by a real and understandable love for a machine which had worked true and reliably for so long and had been the only present she'd ever got from the husband it had always looked to me like she loved.

"It wasn't long before Ed Oscar came back with some old mule line."

As I watch her talk, it is her certainty that astonishes me almost as much as the crazy tale she tells. Her plain face shows not the first sign of misgiving, no qualm anywhere. Meddling into the lives of her kin, directed by what she believes is for the best, is her calling, and I wish for a second that I could busybody myself the way she tends the affairs of others.

"Tore loose," she is saying when I turn my attention back to her.

"No," I say.

"Yes, yes, yes!" she screeches. "Reared and pitched when we tried to tie her up with that mule line and tore loose and slithered away from us through the mess of the house and out the front door with as little trouble as a snake in a tangle of vines. I followed, kicking aside and jumping over, but not a sign of her anywhere when I got out on the porch. Then I heard Ed Oscar moaning his customary 'Oh Lord, oh Lord.' I ran back through the house to see what now, and there she was *in* the machine. Sitting waist deep in all that muck and fester, gripping the tub like she was expecting the thing to go spinning off into the sky.

"Oh! I dreaded what we had to do, and was this close to leaving the situation like it was. Lester had been saying to me to mind my own business, and when I pictured in my mind me and Ed Oscar actually hog-tying her and, right alongside that, my own business, I was tempted to just forget it. But I'm a woman who wants to help if she can. It's my belief if you know what's wrong and can make it right, it's a sin not to do it."

Now she has lost me. A moral—simplistic, inserted, all of the evidence not given—leaves me back with the cousin in the machine, holding on. I linger there where she has crawled into her washing machine. Her mind staying where her happiness was, reality reaching to grip her heart. I know the place. I was there once. I see my own hands gripping the sides of a little boat which slides over the deep, black, wide waters of a millpond. I sit up front in the bow, and Daddy is behind me at the till of the noiseless, battery-powered motor. We knife across the surface of the pond, our wake spinning out from the point of the bow. The place, this pond is to me the world of water, for here, every watery thing is. The dam is no wider than a garden gate, and water spills quietly over its algae-slick edge like a silk scarf sliding off a polished table. Down below, the old mill wheel lies wrecked, draped with Spanish moss as if long ago a paddle-wheeled steamer had gone over the dam. The dark uninterrupted middle of the pond is my ocean. Around the edges, the bushes hide the seam between bank and water like upholsterer's fringe and the trees hunch over, their leaf-heavy limbs limp as if just having rinsed themselves in the pond. Bay blossoms scent the air tropical. When we go there in the boat, I pretend we are exploring a jungle river. There is a tiny bay far off around a jutting stand of live oaks which is all stumps and dead trees lacy with gray lichen and little green explosions of mistletoe. This is swampland, vast and infested with all the water monsters I can imagine. Turtles, baking in the sun like rounds of bread, are lined on half-submerged logs.

I have never been here before this day, and it is as we glide around the pond looking for the perfect place, which only my daddy knows in some secret way is the place where we can catch fish, that I begin to enlarge all that surrounds me. Impressions form gradually, take shape slowly, and other things appear and have meaning instantly, as if God had had a whim to make a tree or a shadowy bank where just before there had been nothing. Or so that first real look at trees and water and light appeared to me then. Things came to have meaning that day. It was such a surprise, like getting a joke or falling in love.

But my mind crowds up with separate times and truths and the voice of that woman over there.

I go back to the pond where the sun shines. I am two people, who I was and who I am, there and here, young and old, finding out and knowing already what is happening. Where around me my own private myth is forming. And we float, Daddy and I in his boat far out in the middle of his secret fishing pond, Mother on the sunny bank reading. Now she looks up, and even from where we are we can see her smile. "Don't take him where I can't see him," she calls. She waves and worries too that I will fall in or we will go too far. And he replies, "No, honey, I won't."

This is the time between loss and memory. The only present my childhood will have. It is a happy day. The day called One of These Days has come.

I had, before this day, only watched as my daddy made his preparations for fishing, a careful ritual, its sequence and accoutrements always the same. Often I have stood by, jealously watching him go back and forth at his steady, unhurried pace between his pickup truck and the shed where he keeps his tackle, ice chests, and bait buckets. I have tried to let him know that I want to go with him. I have never begged, made a tearful plea or even a simple request to be taken along. For the private place to which he retreats as he gathers together his fishing tackle is not somewhere I am invited. I have stood and observed, and from outside his attention, learned how to behave. There is intimacy here between him and his passion, and to intrude or ask to be included or offer help, even, would be as unacceptable, as impossible as trying to invade someone's sorrow.

"I'd like to go fishing sometime" is all I have ever said. I try to sound dispassionate, and do, I think, for if he sees that I am sick with hopefulness, he doesn't show it.

"One of these days" is his reply. And he goes on with his preparations, which are careful of purpose, economical of movement, worked out over his fishing life so that he does not exert himself by a blink of an eye beyond what is required. The equipment is not abused or even handled one time more than is needed to get it in order and loaded. He goes quietly about his work. His face is calm, and I always wonder where his mind floats at these times. I can only say he is fishing and not fishing. I will come to hear someday of states of grace and perfect harmony and when it is explained to me, Daddy-getting-ready-to-fish will be the illustration my mind supplies. And when I am not on the mind of the one I wish to be, and I have that feeling I get of always being left out for the rest of my life from everything, it is the same sadness I felt watching Daddy get ready to go fishing that overtakes me.

But back. Back to that morning which rushes to me here by Pete's grave. Rushes toward me as my mind winds back until that morning nestles inside this afternoon like an object the same shape as the box in which it is stored.

This morning, suddenly and without explanation, One of These Days came. It began before light, before I woke up. I was dreaming somebody was shaking me, and I woke up and my daddy's face was so close that it was all I could see.

"Want to go fishing?" he asks. I am not so happy I think I am still dreaming. I am so happy I wonder if I am dead. I flip up from the bed like a corpse with a sudden contraction of remembering muscles and kick the covers off me as if they were on fire. Yes, I want to go, and I am happy, and that is uppermost on my mind, but with me all the time, preparing for that day far off then, but here now in the graveyard, when not only would I want to remember the day my daddy took me fishing but interpret it, attaching the meaning to the happy events, is that part of me which notices, has noticed, orders the present as clearly and calmly as if it were recalled. I see Daddy's prideful grin, and it tells me what I long to know but also fear, that he is happy with me for wanting so much what he is able to give me. I cannot fail him, and I can never want more, and the happy boy twists free and jumps out of bed, runs to the kitchen to tell his mother, who knows already. Carefully, she wraps sandwiches. She folds and tucks them in waxed paper so tightly that they will have to be torn open.

"Can you believe it?" she asks when she sees me. We are more accustomed to being left out of Daddy's fishing trips. We are left out of most of his affairs. We grin at each other, Mother and me, for it is not just the two of us who have never been allowed to go fishing with Daddy. His friends at Berenice's are never asked. Not even his best friend, Red, has ever been with him. It is his pond, and he fishes there alone. It is all he has left of his father's property, that and the cemetery. Two useless pieces of real estate. Nearly all the land has been sold, and I suppose we live as we do on the money it brought. He has installed a gate across the path to the pond hung with a No Trespassing sign. Since he is the only one who fishes there, I have always figured the pond to be squirming with fish. I, like my mother, don't eat fish. So, although he must catch garlands of them each time he goes, he never brings more than two fish home, which my mother cleans and cooks for him. Mother and I have already eaten when he, smelling of pond water and beer, comes back after dark to a washed and wiped kitchen, but after Mother has cooked the fish and set one place at the end of the kitchen table, we always sit down again and watch him eat what he has caught. We enjoy his zest for fish and say little while he eats, smacking and sucking, cleaning the bones so thoroughly.

Sometimes, if the beer has not made him suspicious of us, he will tell a little of what can happen fishing. Minimal stories of lines tangled or caught on submerged branches, a snake draped from a tree limb, or of a fish hooked then lost, snagged and out of the water swinging toward the boat then whipping itself free. He says a fish like that starts swimming in the air above the pond and is gone so fast it's like you never had him. These meager reports have always been enough to make me want to go with him.

And something else that I sense happens to him when he's there. He returns different from how he was when he left. I hardly know what I imagine it to be, but I know it is closer to what I think a daddy should be. Nothing extreme, just still and comfortable. His eyes lose for a while that deep look of suspicion, not so gray and tightly watching, and the blue of them then, I like to think, is from seeing the sky in the water all day. When he comes back that way, I don't fear so much what I might see in his eyes when he looks at me. They look to me as if they don't see what the mean part of him tells him he sees, but these eyes that have gazed all day long at the cork bobbing on the surface of the sky, which, reflected, is the surface of the pond, blue and sometimes mapped with clouds, have practiced for a while seeing what is there, and for a time, sometimes no longer than the rest of the night, it seems to me that he looks on his house and my mother and me as a place and people to which and to whom he returns, and I think sometimes I sense something safe around us all, not pride certainly or even satisfaction, but he sits loose and tired, saying nothing, just a part of the room like here is where he is meant to be.

So I want to go fishing with him, because then we will have been there together, and I at least, after I have been, won't have been left out, maybe not so strange to him, and he to me, if only for just while we're there, because my hope is this. That if you are with a person in a place where he is better than he usually is, even if you are just standing by, well, you've seen him in that place, and how he is, and he knows you've seen it, and he has to do better then, even when he's away from the place, and you've got to let him. That's my magic. If I have any, that's my religion.

So, I'M GOING. That is what I kept trying to believe as I stood there in the kitchen that day before light. But each piece of the dream kept happening just as it should, so that as the minutes passed, I became more sure that it was coming true.

First, breakfast—grits and ham and salty eggs scrambled in the grease from the ham, toast the way we all love it, buttered first then cooked crisp in the oven, everything hot and enough of it to last us until the sandwiches. They gave me half a cup of coffee topped off with evaporated milk. I was warm and as awake as if it were Christmas.

"Eat every mouthful," Daddy said. "We might not have time to eat if the fish are biting." I pictured us frantic with lines and bait and pulling in fish enough to sink the boat. I wondered if I might fail him, lose my nerve or make some hopeless, stupid mistake and he would see that I was not a fisher. I kept my eyes on Daddy, watching for instruction, quickly training myself to do as he did. I practiced his movements, picking up my fork, taking a bite of food, spreading jelly on my toast, sipping coffee at the same time he did those things, and I did my best to copy his movements. When his plate was empty, mine was, and then he got up from the table, and I did too and was pleased that I could become like him. But then he looked at me and smiled, and I had to be myself. His eyes darted back and forth, and he glanced off to one side of me as though several things were going through his head at once, perhaps the familiar list of all the things he took with him, or maybe a separate list of new or different things he might need since we were going along. I waited, ready to help.

"We need more bait," he said. "I got some crickets, but they won't be enough for three."

"I doubt if I'll do much fishing," said Mother.

"Still, we need more bait," said Daddy. "You never know what they might be hungry for, so we got to have some of all of it. Crickets I got, and we'll stop at Wiggin's and get some minnows. Those are for the big ones, but what else we need is some worms, some big old fat worms for those old lazy ones that want something different from what they can get where they are. Bait for the ones with a taste for something that comes from somewhere else. You know where you can dig up some big old fat earthworms?"

I knew where. I had killed so many burying my dead animals. Cut them in two with my grandmother's spade, and watched one half squirm with what looked like outrage and the other half draw into the earth, whether to die or grow whole again, I do not know. Or, digging with my hands, scooping out the loose dirt, I would gather up tangles of worms, and with not a sliver of remorse, fling them aside from the shade of the washhouse out into the sun, to either parch or bore for their lives into the dry hard ground there. Hundreds of the slimy, precious things I had wasted. Never knowing that I would want them.

"No," I said. "I don't know where to dig for worms. Can't we buy them at Wiggin's?"

"Sure," said Mother. "We can do that when we stop for minnows. The worms will be my treat. I'll buy them for my men to catch me a fish with."

Daddy shot Mother this look that might just as well have been a slap across the mouth. "Men?" he said. "There's one man in this house, and he says, goddammit, that we need some goddamn worms and that the goddamn boy is going to find them."

I was afraid to move, afraid of what he might do. Mother and I had done something that had changed his mood, made him decide that we weren't worth the trouble it would be to him to take us fishing. He could be that way, change his mind and get all mean of a sudden and without warning because of one little word you'd said or a look on your face that you didn't even know was there or for something you hadn't said that in his mind he thought you ought to have said. It wouldn't matter what was waiting or what preparations had been made, what money had been laid out, you could be dressed and ready, but the thing that was to happen, which you were looking forward to, and which he had promised to do, would be off. It had happened to me, and I had seen it happen to Mother again and again. He was not only immovable but dangerous. It was meanness mostly, but I also saw a look of disappointment, as if what had started out fine and might have been on the way to being perfect had become flawed and therefore not worth it to him anymore. We, Mother and I, had learned to assume we were at fault. Sometimes I could charm away his meanness, but most of the time any effort to improve his mood or try to figure out what was wrong would only make it worse. For weeks after I had stolen the money from Mother's Avon case to go to the fair with Johnny, Daddy blamed me and Mother, when of course the whole thing had been his fault for not being there to take me. We tried everything. I took my beating, the strokes of which were punctuated by his enraged gibberish. "Don't never do nothing I don't let you do" was scanned by the crack of his belt on my legs. It was too senseless a thing for me to hate him for saying, but not too senseless to fear. Mother took the blame. Then we tried to be so good. Then we tried just to be quiet. We tried being pitiful, but it just got worse and worse. When he was away was the only time I felt anything near to safe, and Mother and I lived as though our lives took place during the interval between the last tick and when the bomb explodes. Only he went off and reset himself over and over again. Then one day I had to ask him for a dollar to pay for my school picture. I came up with this.

"Daddy, can I have a George?"

How did I think of it?

"What?" he asked, his face thawing.

"You know, a dollar. For my school picture," I said. He laughed out loud.

"Well, here," he said, getting up and reaching into his back pocket to get his wallet. He gave me the bill gladly, as if he were buying, for a dollar, something he would have paid a hundred for. "Let me give you one."

I tried hard that day in the kitchen to think of something funny like that to disarm him, but I couldn't. What I did do was small and cowardly. I joined him against Mother. I turned and looked at her as though I thought she was stupid and hateful. "Yeah," I said. "Daddy's the man here." Hoping not so much that my remark stung as much as his had, but that he might think it had. Pretending to hurt her to make him think I could be like him. Here in the graveyard after all those years, it is a memory that still lashes.

Mother went back to wrapping sandwiches, but I saw some tears fall from her face and bead up on the waxed paper.

Then, Daddy smiled as if a line of credit had been extended on his patience and good will. He came over to me and put his hand on my shoulder.

"Let's go find some worms," he said. "I think I know where some are. We'll dig them together."

I FOLLOW HIM OUT of the kitchen into the yard. The sun shines, caught in the limbs of a tree in the woods across the field in front of the house. We walk across the untrampled, crusted dew sparkling in our grass. Out here in the cool morning light it seems as if nothing else can happen to threaten the day. I look back at the house, and see Mother standing at the living-room window, still as a picture, her arms folded tight across her stomach. She looks cold and worried. I wish she wasn't watching. It would all be all right if she wasn't watching, is what I am thinking to myself. I want to go back and tell her everything will be fine, but I can't go back because Daddy is walking so fast. I move my hand into the backward arc of the arm next to me and catch his hand in mine. I hope Mother notices this. It is for her that I have done it. To try to tell her it will be all right. That I hadn't meant what I'd said to her. But maybe seeing me like this with Daddy just makes it worse on her.

We walk that way out of the yard and start toward the center of town. We pass the houses on our street, which are glazed with an early-morning, honey-gold light. No one is out yet, and we meet no cars. Daddy takes his hand from mine, and we walk along silently for a while. I look up at him, and I see a thin raised white line, a scar just under his chin which is not visible looking at him from the front. I have the same one under my chin, which I got from a fall when I was learning to walk.

"I got a scar like that," I say, pointing up as we walk along. But he just stares straight ahead.

When we get to the end of our street he still has not said anything, and I wonder where we are going to find the worms. He has that tight, gray, suspicious look that the beer gives him.

"Shouldn't we be going to the woods?" I ask.

"There's a place closer by where I want to check first," he says. And he turns and starts up the Avenue toward where Grandmother lives. I don't follow him at first. He takes a few steps, and when he sees I'm not coming with him, he turns and takes my hand. He is not holding my hand the way I held his. I held his in a grip that could be broken. I couldn't get away from him now if I tried. Soon I can see Grandmother's front yard. Something is not right about this, and I don't want to get to her house. But this feeling I have doesn't make the distance or the time it is taking to get there less. I mostly keep my eyes on the sidewalk watching the lines scroll down as we walk along, but each time I look up Grandmother's yard seems just as far away as it did the last time I looked. Inside me, I hear myself saying, "Oh, oh, oh, no, no, no," in rhythm with our steps toward Grandmother's house.

We go into the yard. He is pulling me now. I have stretched out behind him as far as my arm will reach. In my shoulder socket I can feel how useless it is to resist. His will burns in the joint. He drags me around behind Grandmother's house to the washhouse where my secret graveyard is. His hand is tight around my wrist. He kicks the orange crate with the brick on it, and the bright morning sun shines on my secret.

"Let's see what's buried here," he says. I look up at him, but his hard face stares down at the tidy little flower-covered mounds. "Dig!" he shouts so loud that the tin on the washhouse roof rings.

"No, Daddy," I beg. "Please." He pushes me down, and I try to crawl away from him, but he grabs my belt and drags me back. The damp seeps through my pants. My knees are wet and cold. All I can see is the ground sliding past and then the little graveyard. I scramble away and run into the washhouse. I wedge myself behind the sink, but he claws me out of there, and takes me right back. It is not that I don't want to dig up the graveyard, it's that I wish I had never made it to begin with. I feel as though he has seen me always, whenever I have done things I don't want him to see, like doing Mother's hair or dressing up in her clothes. And this must be true. As he drags me back to that little patch of ground, he says as much.

"How come you thought I wouldn't know?" he says. I don't know how I thought that now. He slaps me on the back of the head. My eye sockets throb, and I hear a siren, and then I go down. "Dig," he hollers again.

I start in, scratching at the dirt with my hands. I am digging like a dog, throwing the dirt aside as fast as I can. I hear a yelp come out of me. Soggy pieces of cardboard break apart, and an eye-watering smell floats up as I uncover fur and feathers and decaying flesh, then bright objects, the metal studs and colored glass and pearl buttons which I took off the toys Daddy had given me. I try to dig without turning these out, hoping Daddy will not see them, but he does.

"Is that what you did with the things I brought to you? Tore 'em up like that to play out here hiding behind the washhouse, like a crazy little girl," he says.

I keep clawing, churning up the earth. Things fall back into the hole, pieces of cloth and the carcass of a mouse, and when that happens Daddy makes me pick them up and throw them aside. "Clean it out," he says. The end of a cigar box shows in one wall of the hole. "Pull that out of there," he shouts. I do, and place it beside the hole. I see his shadow, which had been still and shading me, move, and out of the corner of my eye, I see his foot. He kicks the cigar box and it splits open. The little dead bird inside tumbles out, its wings opening up from the force of his kick. It skims across the grass as if flying. I keep digging until there is nothing left, just an empty hole the size of an orange crate, and yes there are worms humping, squirming, some only half exposed, one end flipping around in the light, the other boring slowly back into the dirt. I straighten up and stare into the hole, then for the first time, I look over my shoulder at Daddy. I am tired, but he looks more tired. He is breathing through his mouth and his eyes are narrow and seem to be looking at nothing. I stand, and this time he does not push me down. I go into the washhouse and find an empty coffee can, then I come back to the hole. I fill the can halfway with some of the black damp soil and start collecting worms.

I don't look back at Daddy, but concentrate on what I am doing, keeping count in my head until I have fifty worms. I turn and hold the can out for him to see. He only glances into the can, then looks away.

"Can we go fishing now?" I ask. His head snaps back at me, and every place on my body gets ready to take a blow. But instead of hitting me, he bends down and takes me by the shoulders.

"Yes, we'll go," he says. "But don't never try to hide nothing from me again. You can't, so don't try."

It is a relief to hear this, and will be, I suppose, for a while. We walk back home side by side. I am carrying the can of fishing worms, and he stays close by, even places a hand on my back when we cross the street. Anybody watching from the windows of the fine old houses on Grandmother's street would think the two of us a sweet sight. As we walk back home, some of our neighbors who are coming out of their houses wave and call friendly greetings to us.

WE DID GO FISHING that day, and it was bright and happy with fresh winds and the boat skimming. Mother read on the bank and Daddy was careful and slow and showed me what to do. How to bait my line so the fish would have to take the hook in its mouth. We ate our sandwiches under a tree on the bank, sitting in fresh green grass with bees bumping all around and the warm sun outside the shade of the tree so bright that the world around the pond seemed to ache with light. After lunch, Mother went out in the boat with us, sitting in the middle with Daddy at the stern and me right up in the point of the bow. We caught fish after fish and could not keep bait on our lines for the gobbling and pulling that was going on down below the sparkling surface of the pond. Mother squealed like a girl every time Daddy's or my line would tense, and, like a band saw, cut a crazy pattern in the water. And when the fish would burst up into the light all flip and shimmy, she'd clap her hands and whoop. We'd put them in the fish box filled with pond water that Daddy kept on board, and Mother would peep in carefully, almost fearfully as if the box were filled with snakes, jumping back every time a fish would make a sudden movement, splashing water on her. We fished until the sun was netted behind the line of trees on the west bank of the pond and the birds began to loop in the powder blue tent of sky over the water, home from what seemed a faraway place. Then Daddy put two fat brims on his string and poured the rest of the catch out of the box over the side of the boat. We went home and Mother cooked his fish, and as usual, we watched him eat them with polite, mystified, good-natured disgust as though we were tourists at a foreign table watching somebody eat what we would not.

So I remember it in the end as a happy day, just as I had started to remember it a while ago, before I thought about what happened in Grandmother's backyard.

"HAVE YOU been listening to me?" the woman asks. "I don't believe you have. You been sitting there, but you ain't been listening. Smiling part of the time when there wasn't anything to smile about, then looking like a whipped dog part of the time, even during some of what was funny."

I tell her I have heard most of it. "It reminded me of

something that happened to me once, and I got to thinking about that for a while," I tell her.

"Well, I'm not trying to remind you of anything, son. I'm trying to *instruct* you," she says, impatiently.

"I've been listening. I'm listening," I say.

She reaches into her décolletage and pulls up her strap. When she does this, her skirt rides up over her knees, which are like two white, peeled potatoes on top of her tanned shins. Then she yanks her skirt back down. These are not shameful or suggestive movements. She could be making a bed she hadn't slept in. She looks straight at me as she makes these adjustments. She's like a fussy bird that knows what feathers are out of place without having to look. Her face shows nothing but her features.

"Well, anyway," she says. "That cousin of mine got out of the state hospital in about a year. Let out is more like it, for at first she wasn't a bit less crazy. Just calmer and fattened up some. I went with Ed Oscar to pick her up. She was standing by the gate in the same dress she'd been taken away from home in, washed and ironed, however. And she was clutching a brown paper sack containing a hospital gown, comb, toothbrush, a little tube of toothpaste and forms that certified her as incompetent and mentally disabled to work on the farm, which entitled her to seventy-five dollars a week in welfare payments. And with the first check, what did she do but cash it and nothing would be right until she had convinced Ed Oscar to take her to Cline Brothers' to see if they had sold that wringer washing machine. Which, of course, they had not. They had set it out behind the store hoping to sell parts if anybody ever needed them, which nobody had nor ever would unless they wanted to open a washing machine museum. She paid them the same price they had given Ed Oscar on the trade-in, ten dollars. Ed Oscar had it loaded onto his truck, and back it came with them. Only she didn't try to start it up or get in it again or anything like we were afraid she would. What she did was she set it out in the backyard, filled the tub with dirt and started planting things in it. Crocus, narcissus, tulips, impatiens, asters, all right with the seasons, and a dwarf azalea that bloomed so thick every May it looked like the thing was making pink soapsuds. Something alive and green in that machine all year.

"And do you know, by jump, if she didn't start to improve. By the time the next crop was coming in, she was right out there in the field beside Ed Oscar working like a man and making sense like one. Taking charge, I mean. Of course she didn't give the money back to the welfare people, which I told both of them was wrong. But it was a sign of normalcy, don't you know. She used that money to buy seeds and plants and fertilizer and a fresh coat of paint every spring for the washing machine. One time after about two years, and she had been doing so good for so long it seemed natural, I asked her exactly what it was that had put her back among the sensible.

" 'Estelle,' she said to me. 'It was a young fellow at the hospital. He wasn't even a doctor yet. Still in school, but helping out around there as part of his schooling. That was all the doctoring we got, those of us who couldn't pay.'

"Well, to hear her tell it, he was wise as Solomon and kinder than Jesus. The gist of it was this. He had convinced her somehow that it wasn't the washing machine itself breaking down that had set her off, but loss in general. Said the thing for her was to learn how to do something useful with her grief over the machine. To lay her grief by, in a place she would know where it was, but outside of herself where she wouldn't be with it all the time and have to tend it twenty-four hours a day. Well, it didn't sound like such a revelation to me, but that's what he told her, and it just proves you get what you pay for. I could have told her what he had. Why, I did tell her. 'Honey, grab hold of yourself.' I said it a million times. But people hear what they hear when they hear it.

"So there it is, and slap me down if she isn't still as sensible as I am. The bottom of the washing machine finally rusted out so it wouldn't hold dirt anymore. Then one leg of it gave way, and it flopped over to one side. I held my breath, but you know, she kept her grip. She salvaged what she could of the little garden she had made. Said she reckoned Ed Oscar ought to haul the machine off to the woods. Then, when she got the next welfare check, she had Ed Oscar take her into town, and she bought a cement sea horse holding a birdbath on its head and put it right there where the washing machine had set. But the garden's still there, see, including the azalea bush. She made as pretty a flowerbed around that birdbath as she'd had in the washing machine. Prettier to me. I rode by there yesterday, and the ground under that birdbath is frothing over with white petunias."

She unfolds her arms and opens her palms in a gesture intended to show that her point is proven.

"I'm glad it all worked out," is all I can think to say. I wish she would go. She doesn't know what's buried here, so I should forgive her for thinking that my grief can be compared to her cousin's hysterics. I won't. She distracted me for a bit, but I am tired—tired of remembering. It's done no good. I can't hold my mind.

The day is nearly over. Long shadows lie back from the headstones, slant over and bridge the graves, connecting my kin one to the other. No shadow falls over Pete's grave but mine. I know what I have to do.

"May I borrow a shovel from you?" I ask.

Her eyes go wide, and it's clear she thinks I've gone crazy. She pulls at her collar. Her hands flutter up to her head and she fusses nervously with her hair, almost as if I had paid her an embarrassing compliment. "What? Well, wait now, I didn't mean. Lord!" she wails.

"It's all right. It's not what you're thinking," I lie.

"You don't know what I'm thinking," she says, backing away from the fence. "First, you tell me what you got buried down there before I lend you my shovel."

"It's nothing," I say. "Just something I hid here, and now somebody knows it's here and I have to move it."

"Took you all day to figure that out?" she asks.

"Yes, all day," I reply.

"Not a body?" she asks.

"No," I say.

"Money!" she shouts, slapping her leg.

I just look at her. I will let her think that.

"And here I been going on about grief and craziness. Why didn't you stop me?" she asks.

"It was a good story," I say.

"Well, I've got one about money and greed, too. If you've got time to hear it."

"No, I'm sorry," I say, and I am a little.

I follow her away from the graveyard. As we walk across the field, several times she looks back at me and smiles slyly, enjoying, it seems, what she thinks is a secret between us, and I smile back, and I almost want to tell her the truth, all of it. Give her another tale to tell when she thinks it appropriate. If there was time, I might do that just to thank her for helping me. But there is not time, so we go along silently like two people who have trudged this way together often.

Up close, her yard is tidy and her home is pleasant. Purple asters and scarlet sage grow starkly up against the white siding of the house. The front porch looks as comfortable as a parlor, with its glider and chairs and pots of ferns. As we walk around back, through the open windows drift smells of good things to eat and of cleanliness. It seems a place to me where two people have had together the life they have chosen. When we get to the toolshed, her husband steps out on the back porch. I wait outside the shed, and she goes in. She comes right out with the shovel.

"Estelle, what in the world!" says her husband.

"Nothing, Lester," she replies irritably. "Go back to the bed." He does not move. She tells me he has emphysema. "It won't be long, I reckon, before I'll be standing over a grave," she says, handing me the shovel. "You better mind how you go poking around that old place with a shovel. You don't know what you might turn up."

I know what I will turn up.

I tell her I'll bring the shovel back before I go.

"Just prop it up beside the shed," she says, and she climbs up the back porch steps and, placing her hand on her husband's back, gently guides him into the house.

THE INTERROGATORY SUN is low in the sky as I push the shovel into the crusted grave with my foot and pry up the first load of dirt. Digging up a grave is not like making one. This is careful excavation. I have forgotten how far down I went when I buried the ashes. I know it was not too deep, but inches count here with this tool. I dig a clean square hole about a foot down. Then I skim the shovel along in the hole scraping it out a little deeper. The last digging is on my knees, pulling dirt up and out of the hole with my hands. After a while my fingers scrape metal, and when I brush the dirt away, there is the round, domed top of a canister in the hole like something being born. I uncover more until I can see the rim of the container, then I get down in the hole and pull slowly, steadily, until it gives. There is a sucking sound as it comes out, leaving an impression as near like itself as a mold in the bottom of the grave. I brush it off with my hands and set it on the ground beside the hole. I am leaving the hole uncovered. Daddy will see it, or somebody else will and tell him.

I carry the container to the car, place it on the seat beside me and drive back up the path. I stop at Estelle's and Lester's and prop the shovel against the side of the tool shed, then get back in the car, turn onto the road and start for the airport.

The road is an old one laid out along the curves and bends of Branch Creek, winding for a while, then it crosses a bridge over the creek, straightens out and heads for the highway. I drive along, the light from the low sun flickering through the trees into the car like sparks from a loose wire. Sometimes I look over at the container. Where will I put them when I get home? Pete loved being in this world, so any place will be fine —the sea, the mountains. If he can't rest in that graveyard, it doesn't matter so much to me. But when it is time for me to die, who will bury me? Where will I lie?

We drove like this often, to places we looked forward to seeing. Once all the way across the country. And we were not like the discriminating travelers who pick one destination and leisurely investigate all its attractions. We raced along, skimming the surface, spending as much time moving as staying still. I shall prefer to think of us that way, on the move, seldom lighting, unattached except to each other.

A sharp bend, then a gap in the wall of trees and brush along the road, and I brake the car as though remembering something left behind. I back up and stop in the road beside a path which leads off into thick woods. The path has a metal livestock gate across it hung with a No Trespassing sign. I sit for a minute looking down the road, then I pull over to the shoulder, take the canister and get out of the car. I climb over the gate and start up the rutted path. It is a long walk, but finally the woods open and before me is the pond still and dark. The sky is pale above with only a memory of blue in it, and the trees and brush stand out dark against it, ruching the pond in dark mourning. A perfect circle expands out over the water where something has broken the surface. Then stillness. Then another. I walk to the edge and look down and fish dart out from under the overhanging grass. Some cruise in loopy circles a few feet from the bank. Some hang motionless in the water.

Though it is hard to do, it is not as difficult as I had feared to open the container. I do not look inside but hold the container over the water and pour the contents out. The ashes fall in a gray column and hit the water. Some burst out on the surface of the pond like fireworks in a starless night sky. Some drift down onto the muddy bottom. Sensing the quiver on the water, the fish gather irresistibly like iron filings to a magnet. Some come to the surface and their mouths open and the ashy water goes in. Others go to the bottom and pick.

The water is roiling for a while. Then it is still again. A feeble breeze blows once, writing an epitaph in soft italics across the surface of the pond.

I go back to the car and drive off just in time. In the mirror I see a truck appear out of the bend in the road. It pulls up to the gate. In the back is a small fishing boat. A man gets out, fumbles at the gate, swings it open, and then gets back into the truck and drives through.

It is Daddy.

Come to get in a little fishing before it gets dark.

A Note About the Author

ANDERSON FERRELL GREW UP ON A TOBACCO FARM IN NORTH CAROLINA AND NOW LIVES IN NEW YORK CITY. HE BROUGHT OUT *WHERE SHE WAS* WITH KNOPF IN 1985. *HOME FOR THE DAY* IS HIS SECOND NOVEL.

A Note on the Type

THE TEXT OF THIS BOOK WAS SET IN ELECTRA, A FACE DESIGNED BY W. A. DWIGGINS (1880–1956). THIS FACE CANNOT BE CLASSIFIED AS EITHER MODERN OR OLD STYLE. IT ATTEMPTS TO GIVE A FEELING OF FLUIDITY, POWER AND SPEED.

COMPOSED BY DIX, SYRACUSE, NEW YORK
PRINTED AND BOUND BY ARCATA GRAPHICS,
MARTINSBURG, WEST VIRGINIA
DESIGNED BY PETER A. ANDERSEN